She blamed the ent... shirt.

His shirt, to be precise.

Everything would have been fine, if he'd just kept it on.

But no. He had to go be the gentleman. He'd known she was soaked through. And with no electricity thanks to the ice storm that had blanketed Seattle with hardly any warning, she had also been freezing.

So he'd given her a towel, threadbare as it was, to dry off as best she could.

And then he'd given her his shirt.

Really, that's when all the trouble started.

That's when she'd obviously lost every bit of common sense that she'd ever possessed.

What else could possibly explain the fact that she was now lying on a pile of cushions on the floor of Merrick & Sullivan Yachting with Paxton Merrick's sinewy arm over her waist as if he had every right to do so?

* * *

The Hunt for Cinderella: Seeking Prince Charming

Dear Reader,

It is always fun to revisit old friends, and going back to the world of the Hunts has been no exception. I so enjoyed Cornelia Fairchild-Hunt before, along with her irascible husband, Harry, and giving her an opportunity now to help Shea find her way to happiness with Pax was a distinct pleasure. Equally pleasurable was the opportunity to work on this series again with the incredibly talented Christine Flynn and Patricia Kay.

Poor Shea doesn't know much about love and happily-ever-after, but fortunately Pax does. And once she gives him an inch (or three!) he is determined to show her the way to the mile.

I hope you enjoy the adventure as much as I did.

Best wishes,

Allison Leigh

Once Upon a Valentine

—

Allison Leigh

HARLEQUIN® SPECIAL EDITION®

Recycling programs
for this product may
not exist in your area.

ISBN-13: 978-0-373-65793-3

ONCE UPON A VALENTINE

Copyright © 2014 by Allison Lee Johnson

Printed in U.S.A.

Books by Allison Leigh

Harlequin Special Edition

Silhouette Special Edition

Other books by this author
available in ebook format.

ALLISON LEIGH

There is a saying that you can never be too rich or too thin. Allison doesn't believe that, but she does believe that you can *never* have enough books! When her stories find a way into the hearts—and bookshelves—of others, Allison says she feels she's done something right. Making her home in Arizona with her husband, she enjoys hearing from her readers at Allison@allisonleigh.com or P.O. Box 40772, Mesa, AZ 85274-0772.

For all of you Cinderellas-at-heart

Chapter One

December

She blamed the entire thing on the shirt.

His shirt, to be precise.

Everything would have been fine, if he'd just kept it on.

But no. He had to go be the gentleman. He'd known she
was soaked through. And with no electricity thanks to the
ice storm that had blanketed Seattle with hardly any warning, she also had been freezing.

So he'd given her a towel, threadbare as it was, to dry
off as best she could.

And then he'd given her his shirt.

Really, that's when all the trouble started.

That's when she'd obviously lost every bit of common
sense that she'd ever possessed.

What else could possibly explain the fact that she was
now lying on a pile of cushions on the floor of Merrick &

Sullivan Yachting with Paxton Merrick's sinewy arm over her waist, his big palm cupping her breast as if he had every right to do so?

Shea Weatherby chewed the inside of her lip as she lay motionless in hopes that he wouldn't wake up.

It was morning. Sunlight was filling the room. The wind that had howled and screamed and driven her into his office in the first place in search of shelter when her car wouldn't start was now silent. She couldn't see out the windows without turning over, though, and that was something she didn't want to do.

Because it would mean turning toward Pax too.

Bad enough she could feel the heat of his body burning down every inch of her backside. Because she'd obviously lost her head after the whole shirt-offering incident, she clearly couldn't be trusted to look at his infernally attractive face or other…body parts.

She closed her eyes against the sunshine, wondering how on earth she'd be able to salvage some dignity here.

She'd known Pax for well over two years. Had been regularly turning down his flirtatious overtures for just as long. But all it took was one night, stuck together because her bank account couldn't extend itself yet to replace her old junker of a car once and for all, and she'd tumbled like a house of cards.

He'd loaned her his shirt to wear when she'd been soaked. He'd wrapped his arms around her and kept her warm when the electricity had gone out because of the storm. And when, heaven help her, she'd tasted the brush of his lips…

She wasn't even sure who'd kissed who first, and Shea was more than a little afraid it had been her.

She curled her fingers into the cushion and blocked off the thoughts. Tried to, at least. It was hard, when her body still felt sated and warm and—might as well just admit it—more relaxed than it had been in years.

And more satisfied than ever, period.

Again, she shushed the voice inside her head.

She knew she should be grateful that Pax had been here at the leasing office at all. He spent a lot more time at the company's actual boat works location farther up the shore near the bridge than he did here, at the office that overlooked the marina where the sailboats they leased out were moored. If he hadn't been here, she'd have been stuck sitting inside her car that refused to start and riding out the ice storm because she'd had no way of getting back inside Cornelia's building next door once she'd let herself out. Shea had just started working for the woman a week ago and hadn't wanted the responsibility of an office key when she'd been offered one. By the time the storm had struck yesterday afternoon, everyone else in the office had already left before the roads became impassable, leaving Shea to fend for herself.

She squelched a sigh and opened her eyes again.

Pax had dragged the cushions they were lying on from the boxy, wooden chairs that were scattered around the airy office interior. They were thick and square and covered with a nautical stripe, and though they didn't make an ideal bed, they were better than sleeping on the hardwood floor. It had been either the cushions, or curl up on a desktop. He'd also found a canvas tarp for them to use as a blanket and a few stubby candles that he'd stuck in mismatched coffee mugs to give them a little light.

Her gaze went from one of the de-cushioned chairs to the round table that sat in the center of the room. A showroom, she supposed it could be called, because—aside from the chairs—the only other piece of furniture was that round table, with a massive, wooden model of a sailing sloop displayed on top of it.

Pax and his partner, Erik Sullivan, built boats. Big, beautiful custom sailing yachts that looked like poetry in the water. Both men were single. Both numbingly good-looking. They were part of the yachting world and all that that entailed—money and the "beautiful people." But they both had an interest in the welfare of their community, which was how Shea had come to meet Pax in the first place while covering a story for her newspaper, *The Seattle Washtub*.

It'd just been a human interest thing. Local boys made good—*very* good—by sharing their wealth with a group of kids. Didn't hurt that those local boys were single, extremely attractive and millionaires.

She grimaced and shifted restlessly, and the second that she did, Pax's thumb moved, brushing slowly over her nipple, which traitorously tightened and ached for more. She froze. Waited for another movement from him and wished that she could say that she dreaded one.

But that would be a monumental lie after what they'd already done. What her tightening nerves suggested would be a smashingly good thing to do again.

Shea prided herself on being practical. On being honest with herself. She knew perfectly well that nothing good ever came out of lying to herself.

Or out of weaving dreams from a slanted, sexy smile.

Been there. Done that. And had earned nothing but heartache as a result.

Pax's thumb stroked her again. "You're thinking too much." His voice was deep and rumbling and ridiculously appealing as his fingers slid over her, moving with the delicate precision of a musician.

She slammed a lid over her romantic notions and fo-

cused hard on the base of the table a few feet away from
her nose. "I'm not thinking anything at all."

He shifted, bending his knee into the crook of hers.
Every inch of her skin from knee to neck felt singed by
him, and there was no mistaking the fact that he was well
and truly awake. "I can feel you thinking," he murmured.
"And it'd be much more fun if we just settled on the *feeling*."

If she really were thinking, she would have found some
way to resist him. She wouldn't be yearning, even now, to
feel him moving possessively over her. Again.

She steeled herself against the seductive warmth sliding through her veins and rolled onto her back, looking
up at him.

At the best of times, Pax was impossibly handsome.

At the worst of times, like now, he was even more so.

It was just something about that whole unshaven look,
whiskers blurring the hewn angle of his long jaw and wavy
brown hair tumbling down over his dark brown eyes.

She fought the urge to drool a little and ruthlessly
slapped her palm against his chest, shoving him away as
she scrambled from beneath the canvas. "This was a mistake."

He propped his rumpled head on his hand, managing to
look amused and sexier than ever in one fell swoop. As if
he knew good and well that she was just as hot for him as
he apparently was for her. Or maybe that was simply his
usual state whenever he wakened on a cold office floor
covered in nautical canvas.

"You weren't saying that earlier." His lips stretched
into his familiar, lazy smile. "I definitely remember things
like…more." His voice dropped. "More."

The problem was that she *did* want more.

Which was a bad thing. Capital *B*. Capital *T*.

"I'm not saying it now." Goose bumps crawled over her skin as she moved around the model. She snatched her sweater off the boat's bow where he'd hung it to dry and wondered if it had ever been draped with female items of clothing before.

Knowing Pax, it probably had. The man seemed to have his own set of groupies. Every time she'd done a story—and there had been eight of them now, featuring him or his partner, Erik—he'd been surrounded by beautiful women.

She dragged the damp knit over her head and was glad that it reached her thighs. She'd left her wet bra in the bathroom when she'd changed into Pax's dry shirt, and she was pretty certain that her panties were bunched somewhere under that canvas with him and that darned shirt of his.

She was also pretty sure that now was not the time to go hunting for them.

Instead, she yanked her corduroy pants up her legs, wincing at their cold dampness, and headed to the windows that overlooked the deserted street fronting the ancient brick building.

Her traitorous little economy car was still parked in front. She could see the icicles dripping from the bumper like Christmas decorations. She hoped it wasn't going to cost a fortune to fix whatever had gone wrong this time. Her bank account had just now stopped gasping for air thanks to starting her part-time gig next door for Cornelia.

"How does it look out there?"

"Frozen." She didn't let her gaze linger on him any longer than necessary when she turned away from the icy sight. She already knew he was the exact opposite of icy.

The room was cold. Her clothes uncomfortably damp. But warming herself with him again was absolutely out of the question.

She didn't have one-night stands. She didn't have stands, period. Repeating that mistake was not going to happen.

She picked up the three coffee mugs and set them on the table next to the sloop. "I'd kill for a cup of hot coffee." Better to focus on a craving for caffeine than a craving for him.

"The swill here is stone cold and gonna stay that way until the power is restored." He was sitting up with the canvas wrapped around his shoulders. He ought to have looked silly. He didn't. "We've got the rest of those saltines Ruth kept around, and that's about it."

Her mouth was watering. Unfortunately, it was not for the package of stale crackers that his secretary had left behind before going out on maternity leave.

She shoved her hand through her hair, pulling it back from her face. It felt like a rat's nest to her, but that hadn't stopped him from twining his fingers through it earlier.

Her stomach gave an excited swoop and she swallowed hard, escaping to the restroom. Flipping the light switch in the small room yielded no results, but there was at least enough light from the high, narrow window to see by. The tiled room was clean and neat, and Shea wanted to hide out there as long as possible, but it was too cold. Her bra was just as damp as the rest of her clothes and she balled it up as best she could and shoved it in her pants pocket, unable to face adding yet another damp layer against her skin. She used the toilet, washed her hands in cold water, cringed at her bedraggled reflection in the mirror and reluctantly returned to the reception area.

Pax had shed the canvas blanket and pulled on his jeans. He'd left the top button unfastened.

Her gaze lollygagged over the hard ridges of his abdomen, and she felt her cheeks flushing when her eyes finally reached his.

Definitely, she blamed it all on his shirt.

He was grinning slightly, as if he knew exactly what she'd been thinking, and then he leaned over to pick up the white button-down offender from the floor.

"I need to get home," she announced, her voice abrupt and too loud. "My cat is sick."

He straightened, smiling outright. "That's an excuse I haven't heard before."

"Marsha-Marsha," she prattled, hating the nervousness bubbling up inside her as much as she hated that weird feeling in her stomach whenever she looked at him. "She's sixteen years old. I, um, I have to give her antibiotics right now."

The amusement in his dark brown eyes turned to something else. Something softer. Something unexpected. He pulled on his shirt. "How long have you had her?"

She managed to look away from him and focused on the wooden model ship sitting on the table. She didn't know much about boats, but the gleaming structure looked like it belonged in an art museum. "Since she was a kitten. My, um, my stepfather Ken gave her to me." Ken had been number three in the line of her mother's seven marriages. He was long gone now, but Marsha-Marsha was still here.

"Well, then," Pax said, as if the decision were easy. "You need to get home."

Her car hadn't started the day before. She doubted sitting in a storm gathering ice would have cured its ills. "You think the buses are running again?" Everything had ground to a halt the afternoon before.

His smile was immediate. "Doesn't matter if they are or aren't. As long as the roads are passable, I'll get you home."

Again with the swoop inside her.

She shook it off. "I live on the far side of Fremont,"

she warned. Her apartment wasn't exactly right around the corner.

"I know."

She studied him for a moment. "I don't remember telling you where I lived." Their conversations, outside of any interviews he'd given her, were lighthearted in the extreme, usually ending with him suggesting that her life wouldn't be complete if she didn't go out with him. He'd invited her out for everything from coffee to a sail around the world.

She'd never once taken him seriously. It was simply part of his genetic makeup to flirt with women.

"Just because you get paid to ask questions doesn't mean you're the only person who ever does." His voice was dry.

"Who'd you ask about *me?* Mrs. Hunt?" She couldn't imagine the very elegant, überwealthy Cornelia Hunt gossiping about anyone, even with the ridiculously charming Paxton Merrick. But then again, Shea could hardly imagine Cornelia's unusual business venture either, despite having been a witness to its very birth. The woman had no need to *ever* work because she was married to one of the richest men in the country, yet she'd set up shop to help women succeed in business even when many of them didn't realize they needed help. And now Shea was a minor contributor because Cornelia had hired her part-time to conduct background checks on her prospective clients. At least *she* took Shea's investigative abilities seriously, whereas her boss at the *Washtub* didn't.

"You've got an editor at the *Tub,*" Pax said, as if he'd been reading her mind.

"Harvey Hightower is an ornery old coot who doesn't do anything for anyone unless he's getting something out of it." He called Shea "cupcake" and wouldn't assign her to anything but puff pieces and gossip, no matter how hard or loudly she begged. Didn't even matter that the twice-

weekly independent operated on a shoestring budget. He'd
rather pay a "serious" journalist for the "harder" stuff than
let Shea stretch her wings. He'd decided she was good at
human interest stories and that's where she'd been stuck
ever since she'd started working there after college. But
Harvey *did* love anything to do with Pax and his boat-
building partner because the readers loved anything to do
with Pax and his boat-building partner. Who was to say
that he wouldn't have answered any question Pax asked?

She huffed. "You're an irritating man."

He laughed softly. "Glad to know I'm finally having
some effect."

She grimaced. "Last night wasn't the response you've
been going for these past few years?"

Amusement lit his dark eyes. "I figured it was an early
Christmas present."

"I don't give Christmas presents like that." Truth was,
she didn't give Christmas presents at all, except to her
mother. And that was only a gift certificate to her favorite store because Shea knew there was no point in picking out something personal. Her mother thought Shea had
abysmal taste.

"Well, then. Lucky me." His dimple flashed again as he
grabbed up the canvas and loosely folded it.

It was better to busy her hands than to keep watching
him, so she picked up one of the cushions to return it to
its rightful position on one of the square, wooden chairs.
As soon as she moved it, she spotted her panties beneath,
and she snatched them up and shoved them in her other
pants pocket.

She was pretty sure she'd never carried around all of
her undergarments in the front pockets of her pants. She
was glad her sweater was long enough to cover it all up,
and she pretended that Pax hadn't observed the whole em-

barrassing thing while she put the cushion back in place. The mugs clanked together when he carried them to the break room. With nothing else to do, she sat down and pulled on her leather boots, zipping them over the legs of her damp pants, not because she wanted to, but because the legs were too narrow to fit over the boots. Then she headed to the windows again, peering out.

"Phone lines are still down."

She glanced back to see Pax tucking his cell phone into his back pocket.

"I checked the landline too," he added. "It's as dead as my cell."

"I'm not surprised." She turned to the window again and pointed to the building across the street. A power pole, laden with ice, was leaning against the three-story warehouse. "There's ice hanging on everything." She chewed the inside of her lip. Neither the fact that Marsha-Marsha was waiting nor Shea's desperation to escape would excuse another act of utter foolishness. "The roads are probably still iced over, too."

He closed his hand over her shoulder and squeezed. "We'll get out there and see," he said calmly. "If it's not safe to drive, we won't."

She didn't look at him. It took too much effort trying to ignore the warmth spreading from his hand through her shoulder. "I'm not worried."

"Of course you're not." His tone was desert-dry.

Her lips tightened and she shifted. His hand fell away and it frustrated her no end that she missed his comforting touch. He would forget her the second his gaze fell on another female above the age of consent. It would do her well to remember that.

"I can probably get a weather report on the car radio. Which is more than we can get staying cooped up in here."

He headed toward the back of the office again, and she quickly followed, stopping long enough to grab her purse and her fake-suede blazer from where she'd dumped them. They both were still damp, too.

She joined him at the door on the side of the building that opened onto a covered area between his building and Cornelia's. His red sports car was parked there, protected somewhat from the elements. Beyond the car, she spotted the boats harbored in the marina, swaying in the water. No Merrick & Sullivan boats, though. He'd told her they'd pulled their rental fleet out of the water for maintenance.

"Stay inside while I get it started."

She was glad to. One hint of the cold air outside was enough to make goose bumps sprout on her eyelashes. So she pulled the door closed and waited until she heard the engine running and he gave a quick honk. Then, even though it was his engine, it was still the sound of escape, so she pulled the door closed behind her and ran out to the car. "What about the door? Does it lock automatically?"

"Yeah." Air was blowing from the heater vents with a promising hint of warmth and he was fiddling with the high-tech-looking radio. His profile was sharp and clear and more mesmerizing than she wanted to admit. "Seat belt."

She jumped a little when he glanced at her, then felt her face flush. She fastened the belt. "Cornelia's door locks automatically, too," she blathered. "That's, uh, that's why I couldn't get back in her building yesterday."

His gaze slid over her again. "You mentioned."

She flushed even harder. Right. She'd been full of excuses when he'd pulled her inside his office the evening before. Including the mistakes she'd made in not taking her car to the mechanic when it had started making a new symphony of noises and not *really* believing the weather reports when they warned everyone to take immediate shelter.

She'd just made one mistake after another.

Her gaze strayed to the way his thigh bulged against his faded jeans.

Followed by the biggest mistake of all.

He put the car into gear and slowly nudged out from beneath the overhang, turning onto the street lined with red brick buildings similar to his and Cornelia's.

They drove for three blocks heading inland from the Ballard waterfront before they spotted another occupied vehicle. The heater was doing its job very well now; she imagined her clothes were starting to put off steam. It was a better excuse than thinking she was overheating just from sitting inches away from him inside his hot rod of a car, watching his long fingers, deft and easy on the gear shaft.

She dragged her eyes away and looked out at the icy city, trying to empty her mind.

"You're thinking too much again."

How did he do that? "I'm thinking about how I'm going to get to work tomorrow," she lied.

He snorted softly. "I'll bet you *Honey Girl* that you're not."

She knew that *Honey Girl* was his 65-foot sailboat. That he'd built her by hand. That he'd received offers from around the world to buy her, and that women all over the city jumped at the opportunity to be invited aboard.

"Even if you were thinking about work—which you're not—" he shot her a grin "—I'm pretty certain there won't be anyone working at the *Tub* tomorrow. Listen." He tapped the car radio. "They're still advising everyone to stay off the roads unless it's an emergency."

"Driving me home to my apartment probably doesn't qualify."

"Sure it does." His dimple appeared. "Medical emergency."

"A feline one."

"Doesn't make it unimportant." He stopped at an intersection where the traffic lights were all flashing red and, even as slowly as he was going, the car eased sideways a little. But there were no other cars present. "If my dog Hooch needed medicine every day, you can take it to the bank that I'd find a way to get it to him."

She'd written eight articles about Pax. She knew he'd grown up in the little town of Port Orchard across the sound, where he and his business partner had first started out building boats, that he now lived on the top floor of a luxury building in trendy Belltown and that he had a well-known weakness for anything chocolate. "You never said you had a dog."

"Would you have said yes the first time I asked you out if I had? Or the second time or the third?"

Her ex-fiancé, Bruce, had had a dog. He'd dumped her two days before their wedding.

"No."

Pax watched her for a moment, then continued through the empty intersection. "And what about now?"

"I told you. This was a—"

"—mistake. Yeah. I remember. Why?"

She stifled a sigh. "Because!"

He raised an eyebrow. "Figured a journalist like you would be better in a war of words than that, sweetheart."

"Even if I believed in relationships—which I do *not*—I wouldn't be foolish enough to expect anything from you. And I don't have time in my life to play around." She was busy enough trying to keep her head above water between the *Washtub* and her gig with Cornelia.

His lips twisted. "You always have been hard on my ego."

"Please." She folded her arms across her chest. "Flirting is as second nature to you as breathing. Nothing I could say or do would dent your ego."

"Why *don't* you believe in relationships?"

She exhaled and looked out the side window again. Thankfully, her apartment was only a block away now. "Who in their right mind does? Just drop me at the top of the hill. If my street is icy, you won't make it back up again because I'm pretty sure this little toy of yours isn't sporting four-wheel drive."

"I'll have to let my parents know they're not in their right minds." His voice was mild. "Believing in relationships as they tend to do."

"They're the exception rather than the rule."

"You're what? Twenty-five? Twenty-six?"

"Twenty-eight." And he was ten years her senior. His birthday had been in August, and Harvey'd had her camping outside the nightclub across from his apartment building with her camera to get photos of any gossip-worthy patrons coming in and out. He'd been practically gleeful when she'd shown him the ones of Pax and his dates. As in plural. He'd had three women clinging to him when he'd finally left the club in the wee hours of the morning. It'd been obvious they weren't done celebrating when they'd crossed the street and headed inside his apartment building dragging a bobbing trio of "Happy Birthday" balloons behind them.

"That's still too young to be so jaded," he was saying.

She lifted her shoulder. "I learned early. Wait—" He'd turned onto her street and was creeping down the steep hill. "I said just let me off at the top!"

"And I ignored you." The wheels crunched over the

road, finally coming to a stop in front of her aging apartment building. He rested his wrist on top of the steering wheel and looked at her. "I do that whenever I hear nonsense."

"Whenever you hear something you don't want to hear, you mean."

His lips twitched. "That, too."

Her stomach swayed when his gaze dropped to her lips. She pressed them together and tried not to squirm in her seat. "Whether you want to hear it or not, we shouldn't have, um, you know. Last night. That shouldn't have happened."

"Slept together? Got busy? Had sex?" His brown eyes were filled with devilish mirth. "*Made love?*"

She barely kept from clapping her hands over her ears. "We shouldn't have had sex," she managed sternly. "It doesn't change anything."

He reached out and twined a tangled lock of her hair around his finger. "Don't be so sure about that, sweetheart."

"I *am* sure." She pulled her hair free, unsnapped her seat belt and shoved open the car door. Icy air swept in, overriding the car heater's efforts, though it didn't do diddly to douse the heat inside her. "Thanks for the ride home, Pax, but save yourself some time and look elsewhere for your next conquest. Lord knows there are plenty of women waiting to jump at the chance." She grabbed her purse and leaped out of the car, shoving the door closed again before he could say anything else.

She hadn't even begun picking her way across the icy sidewalk to the building entrance when she heard the whirr of the electric window going down behind her. "My parents are having a Christmas party on Christmas Eve. You should come with me. We can start off at my place with a drink."

Exasperated, she looked back at him. "Pax—"

"I told you I ignored nonsense when I hear it. I'll call you." Then he gave her that trademark half smile of his, rolled up the window with another whirr and drove back up the street that, by all rights, a car like that should have never been able to climb.

She blew out a shaky breath. "Darned shirt."

Chapter Two

February

"She's there."

Pax looked up from the contract he was reading. His secretary, Ruth, was standing in the doorway to his office. "Excuse me?"

Ruth raised her eyebrows knowingly. "Shea Weatherby," she said with exaggerated patience. "I just saw her head into Mrs. Hunt's building next door. Don't pretend you haven't been waiting for her. You'd be over at the boat works if you weren't."

Pax's fingers tightened around his pen, but he still looked down at the latest contract that Erik had landed as if he had all the time in the world. "Thanks for the heads-up."

Ruth let out a sound, half disbelief, half annoyance and all Ruth. "Play hard to get if you want. It's Valentine's Day, so my mother is babysitting the kids and I'm leaving early to have dinner with my husband. I'll come in tomorrow to finish up that schedule for the sailing camp this summer."

He wasn't worried about the schedule. He knew that she would cross every *t* and dot every *i* the same as she always did. "Just don't go getting so romantic tonight you end up needing another maternity leave."

Ruth laughed and walked away.

He waited until she closed things up for the day and locked the front door on her way out. Then he dropped his pen and turned away from the contract that he hadn't been able to read a word of and shoved his hands through his hair.

It was like this nearly every Tuesday and Friday because those were the days that Shea went by Cornelia Hunt's office to pick up or drop off her latest assignment. The fact that this Friday also happened to be Valentine's Day was moot.

Also moot was trying to pretend that he wasn't going to go next door and bum a cup of coffee off of them. Pretty damn pathetic that it was the only time he had a hope in hell of exchanging a few words with Shea Weatherby.

Sleeping with her during that ice storm before Christmas hadn't changed a single thing where she was concerned. She still gave him the brush-off. It hadn't changed a thing where he was concerned, either, except to cement even more firmly what he'd already known.

That he wanted her like crazy.

He had from the very first time she'd approached him with her notepad and pen, looked up at him with her enormous blue eyes and her long blond hair blowing around her shoulders in the breeze, and asked if he minded if she recorded their interview.

He'd looked into those eyes and felt the world stop. He'd thought that the heavens were really smiling on him when he'd learned that she'd be regularly doing some work for Cornelia Hunt next door. And then that his chances with her were looking up after that ice storm. He was a man used to getting what he went after and one night wasn't enough.

But she had remained stubbornly resistant. She'd slept with him, yes. But she'd refused to see him again. Period.

He knew it wasn't because she was uninterested.

So much of her was a mystery, but that wasn't. It wasn't arrogance or conceit that made him believe it, either. They'd been pussyfooting around their attraction for a good two and a half years, but the night of the ice storm, he'd hoped that they'd finally stopped playing.

He hadn't even intended to do anything that night but keep her safe. The storm had stopped the city cold. Bridges and roads had been closed. Erik had been stuck out in Port Orchard and Pax had been at the office to take care of some paperwork. He'd seen Shea's car parked in front of Cornelia's building and so he'd waited around. Then, when the storm descended in earnest and her car hadn't started…

Of course he'd given her shelter.

Only she'd kissed him. And given him hope.

After all this time of being shot down by her, she'd opened the door wide and he wasn't the kind of man who ignored opportunities.

He shoved back from the desk, grabbed a coffee mug from the break room and went out the side door, crossing from the alleyway between his building and Cornelia's to her front entrance. He went inside, passing by the discreet plaque affixed outside the door that said FGI.

He hadn't known what the initials stood for until his partner had told him it stood for Fairy Godmothers, Inc. Erik had laughed wryly over it because he'd met his new fiancée through the business and it wasn't a dating service at all, despite the sound of it.

As long as Erik was finally happy having fallen in love with Rory, Pax didn't care if FGI *was* a dating service. But he knew Cornelia's new business was about business—namely, helping give young women a start that they might not have otherwise been able to have.

It was one of the things Pax liked about the older woman. She cared about helping people. And she was surprisingly self-effacing and low-key for a woman who'd recently married one of the wealthiest men in the country, Harrison Hunt. He—and the computer company he'd founded, HuntCom—were household names.

What wasn't low-key, though, was the interior of the building she'd bought several months ago. It had been in a constant state of renovation ever since, but it was clear that the place wasn't going to be your ordinary office building. Now, the entryway was complete with a marble floor with inlaid medallions in the center, spurring a sense of guilt whenever he crossed it wearing his work boots. The space looked more like it needed to be hosting art exhibits.

Not that there was a lack of art in the space. Paintings were hung above the split, curving staircase that led to the upper landing where scaffolding was clearly visible. Pax was no expert on art, but he figured the impressionist paintings were likely originals given Harrison Hunt's insistence that his new wife have nothing but the best.

"Good afternoon, Pax!" An attractive woman wearing glasses was descending the one side of the staircase that wasn't cordoned off with heavy, milky white plastic. "Come for some coffee, did you?"

He lifted the mug in his hand in answer. "Hey, Phil." Then he gestured at the plethora of red roses that were sitting in vases on every available surface, including some of the stairs. "This going to be part of the regular decor for FGI or just a comment on it being Valentine's Day?"

Felicity Granger laughed lightly and plucked a rose from one of the staircase bouquets as she finished descending. She deftly broke off most of the stem, then reached out and tucked the tightly furled flower through a buttonhole near his collar. "Valentine's Day, of course." She looked around at the overwhelming floral display. "Mr. Hunt's doing, naturally." She smiled. "Cornelia tossed up her hands when they were delivered. I guess she figures if she can't control her husband's grandiose interference with the renovations here, she's not going to be able to stop him from buying out half of the floral shops in Seattle." Phil walked with Pax back to the fancy little break room that was better equipped than most kitchens. "I put on a fresh pot to brew when Shea arrived." She gave Pax a sideways look. "I figured you wouldn't be far behind."

He grabbed the pot and dumped some in his mug. "I just came for the java."

Phil nudged up her glasses and shrugged. "Twice a week now for how long? Month? Month and a half? When you have three minutes or so alone with her if you're lucky? How's that approach working for you?"

His neck felt hot. He was thirty-eight damn years old. Had been voted most eligible bachelor in Seattle three different times. Even before he and Erik hit the big time a decade ago after designing a sloop for one of Harrison's sons, J.T., Pax had never had problems finding a date. But he couldn't seem to get a particular short, curvy blonde to take him seriously at all. "FGI isn't supposed to be a dating service," he muttered. If it was, maybe he should consider hiring them to improve his chances.

Phil just laughed again. "Shea's upstairs in Cornelia's office but I'm pretty sure they're nearly finished," she said as she headed out of the break room. "In case you decide you want to try a more direct approach."

Pax had visited the offices at the top of the stairs only once when Cornelia had given him a tour of the ongoing renovations. He damn sure wasn't going to go up there now to hunt down Shea. Instead, he leaned back against the granite-topped counter and leisurely sipped his coffee.

It really was a helluva cup of coffee. And he knew Shea wasn't likely to leave the place without first filling up the travel mug that she always had with her.

He knew the second she was heading down the staircase, not just because he could hear her voice as she spoke with Cornelia, but because his nerves twitched the way they always did whenever she was in the vicinity.

"Good afternoon, Pax," Cornelia greeted when she walked into the small room, her softly lined face looking amused. "What a surprise to see you."

Shea snorted softly. But instead of reaching for the coffeepot, she moved past Pax without looking at him and filled her travel mug with water from the dispenser sitting next to a built-in gas range. "Hardly a surprise when he seems to spend more time here than he does at his own office. Nearly every time I come by, he's here."

Pax saw the way Cornelia pressed her lips together and looked away, trying not to laugh.

Fortunately, Shea didn't notice.

Her honey-gold hair was loose, streaming nearly to her waist. Her short jacket was the same chocolate color as his dog, Hooch. She often wore jeans and boots, but today she was wearing flat-heeled loafers, brown tights and a pleated orange skirt that ended just above her shapely knees.

When she straightened, he quickly looked up from her legs, and her wide eyes collided with his.

She had dark circles under eyes as if she were short of

sleep, but she was still the sexiest woman he'd ever seen. "No coffee today?"

"Not today." Her lashes dropped and she looked toward Cornelia. "I'll get that background report to you right away."

Cornelia smiled, her expression under control again. "I appreciate you putting a rush on this one. Phil found her for us, and we're just waiting on your report to pair her with a mentor." Her gaze took in Pax. "If she turns out to be our next client, I have an ideal match in mind. My son-in-law Gabe is in construction and one of his partners has been looking for a new challenge. I think her business plan might be right up his alley."

Shea nodded, her eyes still avoiding Pax's. She patted the oversized purse hanging from her shoulder and he guessed she probably had an email or a letter regarding Cornelia's latest project inside. "I'll get on it tonight."

"Oh, don't do that." Cornelia tsked. "It's Valentine's Day. You should be out enjoying the evening. Your research can wait until morning."

"I don't have any plans." Shea didn't seem upset at that fact, either. "I'll leave Valentine's Day for the people who believe in all that—" she waved her hand slightly "—stuff."

"Like my so-subtle Harrison?" Cornelia smiled. "He's taken Valentine's Day to a new level, as we *all* can see. The man has no sense of moderation." She patted Shea's shoulder and turned toward the doorway. "Take one of the bouquets on your way out," she invited. "You, too, Pax. You can give it to Ruth or something." She sailed out of the break room.

Shea's gaze flicked up to his, then away again. She moistened her lips. Looked as if she were going to say something, only to shake her head once and tuck her hair behind her ear. "Enjoy the coffee," she muttered and followed Cornelia out of the room.

Pax grimaced, left the coffee mug on the granite counter and went after her. "Shea. Wait."

She stopped, spinning on her heel in the center of the marble foyer. "Pax, don't. Please. I don't have the energy right now."

"Energy for what? I just wanted to say Happy Valentine's Day."

Her lips twisted. "Right." She reached out and touched the rose Phil had stuck in his shirt. "Never figured you for the type who'd get excited over a Hallmark holiday."

He wondered what she'd have to say when she got home and saw the delivery he'd arranged for her. "Valentine's Day predates greeting-card companies. What's got you so tired? Your editor over at the *Tub* putting you on more stories or something?"

"Always plenty of silly stories and gossip." Her foot edged toward the doorway as if she couldn't wait to escape. "I've just been busy."

"Are you seeing someone?"

There was no mistaking her surprise. "No!" Her gaze darted toward the empty staircase. "No," she said more calmly. "I've told you before. I'm not interested in dating *anyone*."

Pax didn't particularly care if they were overheard by Cornelia or one of her employees. It wasn't like it'd be news to them that he was pursuing Shea. "So I shouldn't take it personally that you've been avoiding me even more than usual."

She looked pained. "I'm not…avoiding you."

He had ample evidence otherwise, but debating with her was pointless. "I know you decided somewhere along the way that I'm a player. That I'm not really serious where you—or anyone else—are concerned. But I'm still curious why you're so opposed to—"

"—sexual hookups?" She looked around the foyer that was literally coming up roses. "Please don't say romance."

"I was going to say relationships," he corrected blandly.

"We have a relationship—journalist and frequent subject." She looked ready to say more, but all she did was rock on her heels a few times and tuck her hands inside the pockets of her short jacket. He couldn't see any evidence that she wore a blouse beneath it, which had him fondly recalling the lacy bra she'd worn the night of the ice storm.

"Don't look at me like that," she whispered.

He closed his eyes. Her image still filled his head right along with her soft, slightly powdery scent. "Relationships with anyone outside of your work," he clarified.

She was silent for so long, he wasn't sure she was going to answer. "Because there's no point," she finally said. "They never work out."

He opened his eyes, studying her for a moment. Wondering. And suddenly wanting more things than he wanted to admit. "You remind me of Erik."

Her eyebrows shot up. "Your partner?" She stretched her arm above her head until it was straight. "About this tall. Dark hair. Gray eyes. *Male*. I remind you of him?"

Shea was short, blonde and beautifully female. "Until Erik met Rory in December, he was pretty jaded about relationships. Earned it from a bad marriage. You have one of those in your past, too?"

She didn't look away from him, but it seemed like a curtain dropped down inside her eyes, hiding her thoughts. "Never been married," she said evenly.

But there had been someone. Or something. He'd bet on it. "I've never been married, either."

"I've interviewed you eight times. The subject has been covered to death."

He grinned, wanting to lighten the tension in her expression. "So. You've been counting."

She rolled her eyes, though he noticed the twitch of her lips. Which she swiftly controlled, naturally, being the jaded, tough nut that she claimed to be. Then she exhaled. "Pax, I—" She broke off when the front door opened and Belle St. John, one of Cornelia's newer employees, came in, pushing a cart with several bulging bags of mail on it.

Pax had seen the sight more than once now, so he was no longer surprised by the quantity of mail sent to FGI's post office box.

"Crazy, isn't it," Shea murmured while Belle rolled the cart through the arching doorway beneath the split staircases and into the conference room. "I wrote one article back in October where Joanna Spinelli called Cornelia her fairy godmother for helping finance her break into fashion designing. And out of the clear blue sky, people thinking they deserved a handout began coming out of the woodwork asking her for money. And not just for starting up legitimate businesses, either."

Pax had read every one of Shea's articles in *The Seattle Washtub* since they'd met, even the ones that were nothing more than who was doing what around town, and he remembered exactly the article in question. "Cornelia hadn't even started up FGI at that point, had she?"

Shea shook her head and her hair slid over her shoulders, making his fingers tingle. He knew exactly how silky her hair was. How it felt sliding through his fingers. Draping over his chest.

She was still talking, thankfully oblivious to his thoughts. "Joanna's a friend of one of her daughters. The article in the *Tub* went viral, though, and the next thing we knew, we were getting tons of mail for Cornelia at the paper." She shrugged. "And the amount of emails that poured in for her was even higher. The volume actually knocked out our computer server for nearly a week. The response was just as heavy over at HuntCom, too."

"Doubt the computers over there failed," he said dryly. The international juggernaut *was* computers.

"Right?" She gave him a dry look. "Anyway, Cornelia was already thinking that she wanted to help more people the way she'd helped Joanna, and all that public response sealed the deal."

"FGI was born."

"Pretty much." She looked around at the lavish foyer. "Helps when you're married to a man who gives you sixty million or so as a wedding gift that you can invest right out of the gate. Cornelia's already helped nearly three hundred women start their own small businesses. Everything from yarn shops to B&Bs to law firms." She hitched her purse up on her shoulder. "It's pretty impressive, actually." Belle had reappeared again sans cart and Shea waited until she'd gone back upstairs. "Of course, Cornelia and the others have to read through a lot of ridiculous requests before they find a valid one."

"*Others* being the fairy godmothers," he added. "It wasn't just a term of Joanna's. That's what they call themselves, isn't it? And the women they select for their projects are called Cindys." Erik and Rory had told him that.

She made a reluctant sound. "Cornelia values the anonymity of the women she helps even more than she values her own. So, yes. They're…Cindys. As in Cinderella project."

"But you've never called them that. Not in anything you've written about Cornelia's business, anyway."

"Because the terms are silly!" Her voice rose again and

she jumped guiltily when a voice spoke her name from above them. They both looked up to see Phil standing at the top of the stairs.

"I'm glad you're still inside." Phil held up a colorful, woven key chain. "You forgot your keys again."

Shea grimaced and met the other woman halfway up the stairs. "Thanks. Wouldn't have gotten very far without them. Think I need to wear them around my neck or something." She skipped back down the stairs and headed straight for the door. "See you all later," she called out to nobody in particular before seeming to bolt out the door.

"Another successful effort, I see," Phil told Pax after the door softly closed. "Have you ever thought about just asking Shea *out?*"

Pax exhaled. Before they'd slept together, he'd asked Shea out dozens of times and she'd always refused. Usually with a laugh that said she didn't take him seriously at all. He folded his arms over the fancy, curving banister. "And what are *you* doing tonight, Phil?"

The woman nudged up her glasses and grinned. "I have an evening planned with my favorite salted caramels. Unlike a real date, they never fail to disappoint."

"Now you're starting to sound like Shea."

She descended the rest of the stairs until she was at his level. "Don't give up on her."

Phil was attractive. Single. Somewhere in her early thirties, he'd guess. He'd known her for four months, but he'd never once looked at her *that* way. Never once wondered how his parents would like her or what their kids would look like. Annoyingly, those thoughts always seemed reserved for the elusive Shea.

"I hadn't planned to." He wouldn't mind another dose of encouragement from Shea, though. That ice storm had been nearly two months ago.

With a smile, Phil headed past him toward the conference room. "That's what I like about you, Pax. You're a long-haul kind of guy."

He didn't know about that, but he wished Shea weren't so convinced he was only one-night stand material. He picked up one of the bouquets and carried it back to his building to leave on Ruth's desk. She'd be in the office for a few hours the next day, so she'd still have a chance to enjoy the flowers over the weekend.

He packed up the paperwork that he still needed to review, locked up the building and drove home. Hooch greeted him at the door of his apartment with slathering kisses and then immediately tried to eat the rose. He got the bloom away from the dog, tossed it in the trash, changed into running gear and took the dog out for a run.

Everywhere they passed, he saw the signs of Valentine's Day. Which just reminded him of Shea.

He'd finally had enough, and turned Hooch around for home. "Pretty pathetic, eh, buddy?"

Hooch just wagged his tail and trotted alongside Pax. The dog didn't care where they were or what they did as long as he was with his owner.

Back in the apartment once more, Pax turned on a basketball game, fed and watered Hooch and hit the shower.

His cell phone was ringing when he shut off the water, and he stepped out onto the rug, grabbing it. But it was just the Realtor he'd asked to look into some properties for him, and he let it go to voice mail while he wrapped the towel around his hips and wandered into the kitchen to stare into the refrigerator as if it would magically produce something edible. Last time he'd been out to his parents' place in Port Orchard, his mom had sent him home with a bag full of leftovers, but they were long gone now.

His cell phone rang again, and he snatched it up again, checking the display.

Smiling broadly, he grabbed a beer with his other hand as he answered casually. "If it isn't my favorite prickly journalist. Have you been saving my number all this time, or did you dig it up from one of those secret sources of yours?"

She ignored him. "Thank you for the bouquet."

"You're welcome."

"You knew I'd have to respond somehow," she continued. "That's why you did it."

He twisted off the bottle cap and sat down at the stainless steel counter in his kitchen that had an unobstructed view overlooking the city. Instead of the lights, though, all he saw in his head was Shea. "I did it because I thought it might make you smile," he said truthfully.

"It did," she admitted after a moment. "It's the first bouquet of cat treats I've ever received. Marsha-Marsha thanks you, too."

"My pleasure."

He could hear her soft breathing through the phone line. "Well. I just wanted to say thanks. And happy…happy Valentine's Day."

"Happy Valentine's Day, Shea."

A moment later, he was listening to the dial tone.

Hooch propped his chin on Pax's knee and looked up at him.

"Whadya think, Hooch? Any chance of winning the race if she won't even get out of the starting gate?"

The dog flopped his tail a few times on the floor.

It was as much of an answer as Pax had.

In her apartment, Shea set her cell phone on the ancient steamer trunk she used as a coffee table and pulled

Marsha-Marsha carefully onto her lap. The calico tabby had become increasingly frail over the past year, but she'd still gleefully gone after one of the cat toys from the "bouquet" that had been sitting in front of Shea's doorway when she'd gotten home.

She pressed her cheek to the cat's head and listened to her throaty purr. "How am I going to tell him?" she asked. "I had an opportunity earlier today. I tried then. But I just couldn't." No more than she had been able to tell him just now on the cell phone.

Marsha-Marsha just circled around on her lap a few times before settling down.

Shea chewed the inside of her lip and stared at the coffee table.

Next to her cell phone and the basket that had contained Pax's wholly unexpected "bouquet" sat a blue and pink box.

It was the third home pregnancy test kit that she had bought that day. The results for the third test had been the same as the first two.

Positive.

She'd interviewed Pax a lot of times. Slept with him once. He was outrageous and larger-than-life. She didn't want to like him. But she did. She certainly didn't want to want him. But she did.

And now she was pregnant with his baby, and sooner or later she was going to have to tell him.

He'd either run for the hills.

Or he wouldn't.

She wasn't sure which possibility scared her more.

Chapter Three

"Cupcake!"

Shea looked up from her computer when she heard her editor bellow from his glass-walled office. She saved the article she was writing—a lighthearted piece about a duck that was making his home in an elementary school fountain—and went into his office just as Stu, the most senior member of their team, was coming out.

It was Saturday and half the crew was there working because their computers had crashed yet again the day before.

"Got an event I want you to cover," Harvey said.

"Political scandal? Corporate malfeasance?" She smiled facetiously because the man *never* put her on any such hot topics. "Since Cooper's been out sick, I could do the background at least on that helicopter crash—"

"No." He looked at her over his glasses. "It's a fundraiser for some place called Fresh Grounds." He was obviously hunting for something on his messy desk. "A nonprofit located downtown. Merrick & Sullivan are sponsoring the shindig."

Shea's stomach tightened. She should have known she wouldn't get a break just because she'd come in to work on what was supposed to be her day off. She was being punished for not telling Pax her secret the night before. "When is it?"

"Tonight."

"What if I had plans for tonight? I do have a life, you know."

"No, you don't. No more 'n I do." Harvey finally unearthed the paper he'd been hunting and pushed it across his cluttered desk toward her. "Dressy, so see if you can't beg, borrow or steal something appropriate."

She flushed and picked up the press release. The dress code around the *Tub*'s offices was decidedly casual, and her usual jacket and jeans was more professional than some. "How dressy?" If it was black tie, she'd be in trouble.

"I don't know. Just don't embarrass me, all right?" He looked even more cranky than usual, his bristle-brush gray hair standing out from his head.

"Maybe you should send someone else," Shea suggested tartly. "Someone you pay enough to actually own a wardrobe that wouldn't embarrass you."

"Social scene and human interest," he snapped. "Take it or walk, cupcake."

Since she wasn't entirely sure he was joking, she sighed and took the press release with her back to her desk.

"And get plenty of shots this time," he yelled after her. "Readers love the photos."

She just waved her hand in response. He was always complaining that she didn't get enough photographs when she went out. She wanted to remind him that she was a writer, not a photographer. But considering their meager budget, everyone pulled dual duty.

According to the release, the fundraiser was a silent auction, with the proceeds benefiting Fresh Grounds, an agency that provided affordable housing for low-income families. And it was, indeed, being sponsored by Merrick & Sullivan Yachting.

She traced her fingertip over the edge of the page. The kinds of photos that Harvey would want, she knew, would heavily feature Pax or his partner, Erik. Every time they printed either one's image in the *Tub,* the free paper's advertising spiked and their internet traffic doubled. For Harvey, the two men behind Merrick & Sullivan were golden.

But just thinking about seeing Pax again made Shea break out in a cold sweat. And wouldn't *that* be an attractive look?

She quickly finished the duck article and submitted it, then shut down her computer and gathered up her belongings. The auction was being held at the Olympic Hotel, and that alone was enough to tell her that the dress was definitely more black-tie than not. Which meant she had to go see her mother.

No way could Shea afford a fancy gown. She was still paying off the repairs to her car from December.

Her mother, however, was presently married to a cosmetic surgeon and had a closet full of fancy clothing.

"Get those shots," Harvey barked as she walked past his office on her way out.

If there'd only been a shot to ward off Pax's appeal, Shea wouldn't be in the fix that she was in now.

She dumped her stuff in the passenger seat of her car and drove out to Magnolia, the neighborhood where her mother lived with Jonathan Jones, hubby number seven. The sporty little BMW that Jon had given Gloria for her forty-eighth birthday was parked in the four-car driveway, telling Shea there was no hope of her being able to sneak in and raid her mother's closet without having to actually see her.

She blew out a breath, wondering if it was worth chancing her job and showing up at the event wearing her one and only black dress and deciding that it wasn't. She went to the front door and rang the bell, nervously tapping the toe of her boot in time to the chiming she could hear from inside the house.

Two more rings and the door swung open and Gloria Weatherby Garcia Monroe Nelson Garcia Frasier Jones stood there. Surprise filled her blue eyes, though there was no hope of it showing otherwise in her expression because Botox had been her best friend since Shea was sixteen.

"Shea!" Gloria stepped back, pulling the door wide. "You know you don't have to ring the bell," she chided.

Shea stepped inside and gave her mother a quick kiss on her perfectly smooth cheek. "Last time I didn't ring the bell, I walked in on you and the pool boy doing it on the living room rug," she reminded.

Gloria waved her bejeweled hand in dismissal. "That was years ago. Jonathan keeps me interested enough that I don't *need* a pool boy anymore." She pushed the door shut and padded barefoot into the living room, leaving Shea to follow. "You just missed your brother." She grabbed two empty glasses from an ornate marble-topped cocktail table and carried them into the kitchen. "He stopped by to get my signature on a few things."

"I don't have a brother." But she knew her mother was referring to her former stepbrother Marco Garcia, who still acted as Gloria's attorney even though she and his father, Ruben, hadn't been together for more than a decade. In fact, they'd been married and divorced twice, but Marco hadn't lived with them during either marriage period. Shea's contact with Marco had been limited to a handful of holidays that had always been short on celebration and long on awkwardness. It was the same with the rest of her stepsiblings, too. Seventeen of them in all, and that was just from her mother's revolving door of husbands. "You're not even married to Ruben anymore."

Gloria huffed. "Details," she dismissed. Then she narrowed her eyes and studied Shea. "You look terrible," she said bluntly. "Jonathan could take care of those lines you're getting around the eyes. All you have to do is say the word."

Shea ignored her and dumped her purse on the overstuffed white couch. Her mother loved all things white because it left *her* to provide the only color around. "I came to borrow a dress. I'm covering a deal at the Olympic tonight. It's black tie."

"Work?" Gloria pouted her bee-stung lips. "That's disappointing. You're never going to find yourself a husband if you're always working. Didn't you learn anything from that mess with Bruce?"

"I'm not looking for a husband!" She clamped down on the pang inside her chest. "Just a dress suitable for tonight," she managed in a reasonable tone.

Gloria sighed dramatically. "Fine." She led the way out of the kitchen and up the carpeted stairs to the master bedroom that she'd remodeled just as soon as she and Jonathan had moved into the house a year ago. She crossed the white carpet and threw open the double doors to a walk-in closet that was bigger than Shea's living room. "You can thank your lucky stars that we're still the same size," Gloria was saying as she disappeared into the closet. "Although if your boobs get any bigger you're going to pop out of anything of *mine*. Be glad I'm married to Jon. He'll be able to keep those girls looking good for you."

Shea dropped her arms, which she'd folded self-consciously over her chest. "I don't want anything that sparkles," she warned, stepping to the closet doorway.

Gloria pouted again and placed two of the plastic-protected hangers back on the rack. "Here." She thrust three choices at Shea. "Try those."

Shea took the gowns into the en suite bathroom and closed the door. She rapidly undressed, avoiding her own reflection in the mirrors that surrounded the room until she'd pulled on the first of the gowns. It was scarlet, cut up to here and down to there, and Shea couldn't even get the zipper under her arm all the way up thanks to the tight fit across her bust. She quickly tried the second, a brilliant pink strapless satin that clung revealingly like a second skin, making her wonder what on earth her mother was able to wear underneath it. The third was a slight improvement, but only because it had narrow straps and was a simple black. The skirt had a deep slit up the back, but Shea could zip it up and her chest didn't pop out of the top, so she figured it would do for the hour or so that she'd have to spend at the fundraiser getting what she needed to satisfy Harvey.

She pulled it off, put on her jeans and long-sleeved T-shirt again and carried the dresses out of the bathroom.

Her mother was sitting on the wide bed, studying her nails. "I thought you'd at least show me," she scolded without much conviction.

Shea hung the rejects on their hangers and slid them back into their plastic sheaths.

"Ah. The black," Gloria deduced. "Boring and safe but presentable." She rose and went to a full-length mirror that she pulled back to reveal a hidden jewelry case. "You'll need earrings."

The thought of wearing a pair of her mother's heavy earrings all evening was vaguely nauseating.

Earrings aren't what's making your stomach queasy.

Shea ignored the annoying voice of her conscience.

"Here." Gloria turned and held out a pair of sparkling earrings on her outstretched palm. "I hope you'll take time for once to put on some blush, too. You need the color. Honestly, Shea. You'd be a pretty girl if you'd just put a little effort into it."

"Ever helpful, Mom." Shea took the dress and the chandelier earrings even though she knew she'd never wear them. It was easier to go along than argue. "I'd stay for more motherly advice, but I've got things I need to take care of." She had to admit that her mom was generous with her clothing when the situation called for it. "Thanks for the dress. I'll have it cleaned before I bring it back."

"Don't go covering yourself up with a sweater, either." Gloria followed her down the staircase. "The one thing you've got going for you is your figure."

"It's February," Shea reminded. "It's cold."

"A coat!" Gloria turned on her heel and ran back up the stairs.

Shea wished she'd kept her mouth shut.

A moment later, Gloria returned with a long black coat. "Here." She pushed it into Shea's hands. "Just promise you won't wear it once you're at your little event. If you're going to insist on working all the time, you might as well show yourself off while you're walking through the hotel lobby. Maybe you'll catch someone's eye."

"Mom! What do you want me to do? Advertise that I'm open for business?"

"Don't be so dramatic." Gloria put her hand on her

trim hip. "I'm not suggesting you're a prostitute. A smart woman gets a ring on her finger before she starts giving away her favors. I learned *that* the hard way with your father, didn't I? But do you think I would have ever gotten Jonathan's attention if I'd have been covered from head to toe in black wool?"

"Jonathan was the cosmetic surgeon who did your butt lift," Shea reminded dryly. "And I'm not looking to give away any favors to earn husband number one, much less number seven." She knew the conversation had nowhere to go but down, and it was already low enough. She could only imagine what Gloria would have to say once Shea told her she was pregnant after what was essentially a one-night stand.

Her mother had had a lot of husbands for the simple reason that she claimed not to sleep with anyone before marriage—aside from Shea's dad. That, and the fact that she bored easily. Jonathan had lasted eighteen months now, but Shea figured his time was probably not as limited as it might otherwise have been, considering her mother's avid pursuit of plastic surgery to stave off any sort of natural aging process.

"I don't know how you ended up so judgmental," Gloria lamented. "You're just like your father."

Shea's father lived in Europe with his fourth wife, who was younger than Shea. Last she'd heard, Number Four was trying to get pregnant. If she succeeded, the baby would be Shea's only sibling actually related by blood. The news had come in her only communication from her father in a year—a Christmas postcard. Written and signed only by Number Four, yet she supposed it could have been worse: no postcard at all.

"Not being judgmental, Mom, just stating facts." Her temples pounded and she'd been with her mother for less than thirty minutes. A new record. "Thanks again for the dress."

Gloria brushed her lips in the air near Shea's cheek. "You're welcome." Her gaze went past her to the expensive car that was pulling into the driveway next to Shea's four-wheeled heap, and her smile widened. "Jonathan's back from his tennis game." As if Shea were already gone, Gloria jogged out to greet the dark-haired man who was only five years older than her daughter with a long kiss.

Neither one of them noticed when Shea hastily got into her car and drove away.

If Pax ever met her mother, he'd understand why she wasn't a believer in enduring relationships.

Right on cue, her stomach rolled.

Groaning, she rolled down her window, hoping the cold air would blow away her nausea and wishing that everything else in her life could have such a simple solution.

"That's her, isn't it?"

Pax glanced down at his sister, Beatrice, as she tucked her arm through his. Her gaze was focused where his had been—on the entryway to the hotel ballroom where the fundraiser was being held.

Shea had arrived and was standing there, surveying the room through her digital camera.

"I suppose this is your doing."

His sister shrugged, too innocent for belief. "I sent out a press release or two," she allowed. "But I'm right, aren't I? That's her. The reporter you've been mooning over."

He'd hoped that, with the distraction of the auction, he could get through a few hours without thinking about Shea. Yet there she was. In the flesh and looking like a million bucks. "I'm not mooning." Laughter cackled inside his head.

His sister's eyebrows were situated halfway up her fore-head in disbelief. "When's the last time you had a date?"

He'd been on plenty of dates over the past few years. Casual ones that hadn't tied him in knots at all. But he hadn't been out with anyone since the ice storm.

He wasn't sure what bugged him more: Shea's continued elusiveness, or his unaccountable unwillingness to move on from what even his own common sense told him was a losing proposition.

"Don't you have things you're supposed to be attending to here?" As the event planner, Beatrice had put together the high-brow auction.

She gave him a look. "Please. I'm good at what I do, Brother dear. An event by Beatrice runs as smoothly as a Merrick & Sullivan Yacht cuts through the water."

"Cute."

"I try." She smiled brightly, and he was glad to see it. She hadn't been doing a lot of that since the scumbag she'd been planning to marry had called it off. It was one of the reasons he'd been willing to fork over the sponsorship for this particular event. It was her first project since coming back to Seattle after her fiancé and partner in their San Francisco event-planning business had become an ex in every way.

"Not that I'm surprised," Beatrice mused, "but you never said she was so pretty." She poked him in the side. "What are you standing here for? Go talk to her."

"Did you send a press release to the *Washtub* to match-make or to get publicity for Fresh Grounds?"

She lifted her shoulder. "Why not both?" She reached up and planted a kiss on his cheek, then sauntered away, leaving Pax's attention to return, way too easily, to the door.

Shea had lowered the camera; it was hanging off her bare shoulder by a long strap. The black dress she was wearing just made her hair look more golden and her skin creamier. And even from across the room, he could see the expression on her face directed his way, as if she'd tasted something sour.

Because she'd been tasked with another story like this, or because *he* was there?

"Yo." Erik walked up and shoved a squat glass into Pax's hand. "Get a grip, man. You're drooling on yourself."

"Like you haven't drooled over your fiancée?"

Erik grinned. He was solo tonight for his brief appearance because Rory had stayed home with her little boy who had a cold. "Difference is," the other man pointed out, "I'm getting Rory to the altar. Where have you gotten Shea?"

Pax hadn't admitted even to his partner and best friend what had happened between him and Shea during the ice storm.

"Look sharp," Erik murmured. "She's heading this way."

As if Pax didn't know.

He watched her walk toward them. The gown she was wearing was blessedly simple in comparison to some of the overdone getups that night, but it was still sexy as hell, subtly molding her figure. Her hair streamed down her back, held away from her face by a narrow black band. She wasn't wearing any jewelry; her only accessory was the small notepad she was carrying in addition to the camera.

He lifted the drink Erik had given him and drank down half of it. Probably a good thing that it was only water and not alcohol. Judging by the look on Shea's face, he was going to need all of his wits about him.

"Mr. Sullivan," she greeted Erik first. "Congratulations. I heard you're getting married very soon."

He nodded. "Next week. And I've told you before. It's Erik."

"Will I be lucky enough to get a photo of you and your fiancée this evening?"

"Not this time. Rory's home with our son, Tyler."

Pax heard the pride in his partner's voice. Tyler wasn't Erik's by blood, but that didn't stop him from loving the kid with everything he had.

"A son." Shea's gaze flicked to Pax so briefly he almost missed it. Her smile looked a little stiff. "How old is he?"

"Five."

"And will he be going into the yacht-building business some day?"

Erik laughed. "That'll be up to him." He clapped Pax on the shoulder. "You'll have to excuse me for now. I need to talk with someone."

Shea's eyes followed Erik as he walked away. "He seems different," she murmured.

"He's getting married soon. He's happy."

She finally looked up at him. Her long lashes were darker than usual, but it was the only hint of cosmetics that he could see. "You make it sound so simple."

"It is." He shifted, touching her elbow to guide her out of the way of a waiter bearing a tray loaded with cocktails. He snagged a slender flute of champagne. "With Rory and Tyler in his life, Erik's finally found what he's always wanted." Even though his partner had shunned anything approaching romance since a bitter divorce, he now couldn't wait until the day he and Rory exchanged their vows. He handed Shea the glass and their fingers brushed.

Those lashes of hers quickly lowered, shielding her strikingly blue eyes. She started to lift the glass to her lips, but stopped and looked back up at him. "With him being married soon, will that put a greater load on your shoulders at Merrick & Sullivan?"

"Is that an official question, or are you personally curious?"

She pursed her soft, pink lips. He figured if she had any clue how he wanted to kiss her every time she did that, she'd want to drag a bag over her head.

"Both, I guess," she finally allowed, and he wondered who was more surprised by the admission.

"Our partnership is like any good partnership," he said. "Nothing's exactly fifty-fifty all the time. It ebbs and flows on each side."

Amusement suddenly glinted in her eyes. "That's not quite a direct answer."

"Sometimes Erik takes more of a load and sometimes I do. It always works out because we trust each other and we're equally committed to our business."

"You've been partners for a long time now."

"Twenty years." He smiled slightly. "Some relationships *do* last."

The glint went out as abruptly as a candle flame doused with water. "So you've claimed." She set the untouched glass on the table next to them, lifted her notepad and slid a pen right out of the top of her dress.

He couldn't help but grin. "That's better than a magician pulling roses from his sleeve. Anything else interesting down there?" From his height, he had a stellar view of the top curves of her breasts contained within the square-cut dress. His memory all too easily filled in the details of blush-colored nipples that tasted sweeter than summer strawberries.

Her cheeks had turned pink and she grimaced. "I forgot to borrow an appropriate purse along with the rest of this getup."

He dragged his mind out of their memories with an effort. "You borrowed the dress?"

She looked like she regretted the admission. "From my mother." She clicked her pen once. "What was it about Fresh Grounds that inspired you and your partner to sponsor the auction here tonight?"

"That dress belongs to your mother?" It was a helluva dress on Shea. But he couldn't imagine someone old enough to be her mother wearing it.

"Yes." She clicked her pen again. "The sponsorship?"

"How many times have I told you that all work and no play is no fun at all?"

She just looked at him.

He relented. "Fresh Grounds does good work." The gig might have been Beatrice's first since coming back to town, but he and Erik wouldn't have footed the bill for the event if the cause behind it hadn't had significant merit. "Regardless of whose dress it is, you look beautiful."

Her jaw looked tighter than ever. She clicked her pen again and looked pointedly at Beatrice, who was standing a few tables away having an animated discussion with one of the guests. "Shouldn't you be saving comments like that for your *date* if you expect to get anywhere with her? She's the one who is beautiful."

His dark-haired sister was wearing red and did look beautiful. But what interested him a whole lot more was the look in Shea's eyes.

She was jealous.

He managed not to smile. "You think she's my date?"

Her chin angled, challenging. "Isn't she?"

If she only knew.

"You should meet her." He raised his voice enough for his sister to hear and called her name.

Shea gave an annoyed little hiss but greeted Beatrice with a polite smile when she immediately came over.

Pax put his arm fondly around his sister's shoulders.

Knowing he shouldn't be enjoying Shea's obvious annoyance didn't stop him from doing so. "Beatrice, this is Shea Weatherby." He looked into her blue eyes. "Shea," he drawled, slowly, "this is Beatrice Merrick."

He saw the quick dilation of her pupils. The accusation. "You got *married?*"

His enjoyment screeched to a standstill and face-planted right there on the busily patterned ballroom carpet. So much for briefly thinking he was gaining some ground.

"Beatrice is my sister," he corrected flatly.

The relief that filled her eyes might have been comical if he didn't know just how low her opinion of him really was.

"Bad enough being his sister." Beatrice laughed quickly, brave enough to ignore the sudden tension. She grabbed Shea's hand between hers and pumped it. "I feel like I've known you for ages. After that first article you wrote about Pax and Erik a few years ago, I've followed your work in the *Tub*. You have a wonderful gift with words."

Shea barely heard a word of what the other woman was saying.

His sister.

Beatrice might well be Pax's date for the night, but the tall, stunning brunette was his *sister*.

And while the beautiful woman was all smiles, Pax's expression had turned to stone.

Some portion of her mind recognized that she needed to respond to Beatrice, but she couldn't seem to look away from Pax. "Your brother mentioned he had a sister once," she managed, "but I…I had the impression you lived in San Francisco."

Pax finally looked away from her, staring down into his glass, and Shea swallowed, glancing quickly at his sister.

Beatrice's eyes were the same shade of brown as her

brother's. "I moved back about six months ago." She lifted her shoulder. "Decided that I didn't want to go back to working for someone else, so I opened up my own shop here."

Pax suddenly shifted. "Beatrice is the event planner who put this auction together. She's the one you want to talk to tonight." With a faint nod that was clearly directed only at his sister, he turned and strode across the room toward his partner.

Shea had to fight the urge to go after him.

What could she possibly say right there in the middle of the crowded ballroom?

She was sorry she'd misjudged him?

And, oh, by the way, she was pregnant?

"So how long have you been writing for the *Washtub?*"

Shea moistened her lips. It was an effort to look away from Pax, resplendent in his black suit and pale gray tie. But like it or not, she still had a job to do.

"Six years." It was almost a surprise to realize she was still holding her notepad and pen. "And I should be asking *you* the questions."

"Not really." As if they were longtime friends, Beatrice looped her arm through Shea's and steered her toward the front of the room, where a head table was set on a dais. "George Summers is the director of Fresh Grounds. He's the one you want to talk to."

From the corner of her eye, Shea saw Pax heading for the ballroom doors. The intention in his stride was unmistakable.

Sponsor or not, he was leaving, and she guiltily knew that she was the reason.

"I will," she said abruptly. "I just need to take care of something first." She pulled away from Beatrice and followed him.

Catching him was easier said than done. He was long-legged and didn't have high heels and a tightly fitted gown to hinder him. Only the fact that he was waylaid by an older couple he obviously knew just outside the ballroom doors allowed her to reach him at all.

Since she'd known him, he'd always had a smile in his eyes. Usually a wicked one. But when he glanced at her this time, acknowledging her presence before finishing his conversation with the couple, there was nothing in his eyes at all.

Regret swamped her and she hovered awkwardly nearby until the couple moved off. Only then did Pax turn her way. His face was hard, and her nerves flagged.

"You just going to stand there clicking that pen of yours?"

She flushed and realized she had been nervously clicking the pen. "I, um, I need to talk to you about something."

His expression didn't change. "Like the fact that you actually thought Bea was my *wife?*"

She opened her mouth to deny it but couldn't. "I don't know what I thought!" She stuck the pen behind her ear and moistened her dry lips. "I haven't been able to think straight where you're concerned since—" She broke off and took a deep breath.

"I just told you yesterday that I'd never been married." His voice was low, but that didn't mask his anger.

"Yes, well, people say things all the time that aren't true."

"What do you think I did? Stopped by a wedding chapel between then and now? Or that I've been married all along and been lying about it every time the subject came up? That for the past few years, I've been hiding her locked in a closet?" His lips thinned. "There's nothing about me you don't know."

"I don't know everything about you!"

He waved one hand. "Then do that digging Cornelia keeps telling me you're so good at."

How many times had she fought the temptation to use her sources to learn more about him? He'd never let her forget it if he knew. "Invading your privacy wouldn't be right. And I'm doing a *job* for Cornelia, vetting the requests she gets for accuracy. Because people lie. All the time. They exaggerate, they omit and they twist the facts to suit their situations and their wants." She was guilty herself, still omitting that teensy detail that she was pregnant.

"I don't," he repeated flatly.

She was breathless and felt dizzy, so badly did she want to believe him. "I'm sorry, okay? I shouldn't have jumped to conclusions." She drew in a shaky breath. Cowardly or not, she couldn't make herself tell him the truth then and there while just feet away strangers dressed in fancy clothes bid on everything from free haircuts to a season of sailboat rentals from Merrick & Sullivan.

She leaned against the nearby wall and tried to compose herself. Making a scene in the fancy hotel would infuriate Harvey beyond hope. "I have to go back to my editor with some quotes from you and a few photographs, or he's going to be very unhappy with me."

His lips twisted and he yanked at his tie as if it were suddenly strangling him. "The story tonight isn't about me or Erik. It's about Fresh Grounds."

He'd never refused to cooperate for a story before, and she was desperately afraid he'd choose now to start. She'd have only herself to blame, too. "If you want more people to read about the agency's work, it's going to be because you and your partner's names are attached to the story. And—" she admitted huskily "—I'd sort of like to keep my job. I have rent to pay and all that."

He shoved his fingers through his hair. "I must be certifiable," he muttered. "Fine. You want a few quotes, you can have them."

She hastily plucked her pen from behind her ear and flipped open her notepad. He was obviously still furious.

"Tomorrow," he added.

She hesitated warily when that was all he said. "Tomorrow?"

"I'll give you a few quotes tomorrow." His lips twisted. "That gives you time to get the story in."

Beggars couldn't be choosers. She nodded and quickly stopped when she realized she'd started clicking her pen again. "Yes, but—"

"You want something from me, and I want something from you."

Her stomach lurched, rising toward her throat. "I...I'm not sleeping with you."

His expression went even colder. "You might consider waiting to be asked."

Her lips parted, but no words came out. He'd never made any secret that he wanted to sleep with her.

Until he *had*.

Since the ice storm, his propositions had dwindled to none. He'd invited her to his parents' Christmas party—something she'd known better than to accept. He talked to her when they ran into each other at Cornelia's office. And he'd sent her *cat* a Valentine's bouquet.

What he hadn't done again was ask her out on an actual date. For coffee or anything else. And he certainly hadn't given her that look of his that said he wanted to devour her.

Her stomach churned. She hadn't exactly given him any sort of opening

"I'll pick you up at your apartment tomorrow at eleven," he said flatly. "I want a couple hours of your time."

"But—"

"That's the deal, Shea. You don't get to call all the shots all the time."

"I don't call *anything!*"

His expression didn't change. "Eleven." Then he turned his back dismissively and strode away.

Chapter Four

Shea didn't sleep at all that night.

After Pax had walked away, she'd made herself go back into the ballroom and show some professionalism if only to prove she wasn't a complete failure. She wasn't able to interview Erik Sullivan because, while she'd been interviewing the agency's director, he also left early to be with his fiancée and son. But she'd still come away with more photographs than Harvey would ever want or need, even though she knew the shots he really wanted were of Pax and his partner. She'd only gotten the one photograph of them when she'd first arrived, and it was blurry thanks to her hands shaking the second Pax had spotted her.

When she'd gotten home, she'd given up working on the article altogether and finished her report about Elise Williams for FGI instead. Cornelia was going to be disappointed that Ms. Williams hadn't been as honest about the reason for her financial struggles as she'd thought. Shea, however, hadn't been surprised at all. It just proved what she'd told Pax. People lied. All the time.

She'd emailed the report to Cornelia and then lay in bed staring at the ceiling until well after dawn.

Only then had she gone to sleep.

And naturally, given her usual luck, once she'd gone to sleep, she'd overslept.

Which meant that she was still rushing around the next day like a ninny with damp hair and still trying to decide what to wear when she heard a knock on the door.

She swallowed an oath, catching her panicked reflection in the antique mirror hanging next to the entrance. She was wearing blue jeans, a pink lace bra and nothing else.

She stood on her toes to look through the peephole. Of course Pax had to be right on time.

She went back down on her heels and pressed her forehead to the door, willing her heart to settle down. He was wearing black jeans and a heather fisherman's sweater that made his shoulders look a mile wide.

Why did the man have to look so blasted *good?*

"Give me just a sec, okay?" She knew he'd be able to hear. The doors and the walls in the place were thin as paper. She went back on her tiptoes to look through the peephole.

He was looking straight at her, and even though she knew he couldn't see *in* the way that she could see out, she still felt heat streak through her. She nervously jumped back, nearly tripping over Marsha-Marsha, who'd decided to take that moment to wind around Shea's feet.

The poor cat let out a squall and bolted for her perch at the top of the cat tree near the window.

Pax knocked again. "You okay in there?"

"Yes!" Her voice sounded as frazzled as she felt. She didn't even know what it was he had in mind. She liked to be able to put a name to things, but she didn't know if this was a date, an interview or what.

She just knew that her head was pounding, she felt sick to her stomach and she was a nervous wreck.

She'd never had to tell a man before that she was pregnant with his child.

"I'm fine," she said loudly. "Just tripped over the cat." She snatched up the first long-sleeved T-shirt she'd started out with before having an attack of what-do-I-wear-itis and yanked it over her damp head. Then she grabbed up the pile of discarded clothes, lifted the lid of the steamer trunk and dumped them inside to hide the evidence. She twisted her hair up on top of her head, stuck a long pin in it and yanked open the door.

She was sweaty and breathless and a lock of hair fell over her forehead. "You're the type who's never late, aren't you." It wasn't a question.

"When it's important."

Her shoulders sagged. "I hate it when you say stuff like that," she muttered. It made her feel like she was the worst person on the planet.

"Sorry." He didn't look it as he stepped past her without invitation and glanced curiously around the apartment.

Aside from the occasional girlfriend, Shea didn't invite people to her apartment. It smacked of allowing them too close. This was her space. Her refuge.

"Not what I expected," he said after a moment.

Her muscles tightened. She'd spent a lot of time in a lot of secondhand stores finding good pieces, and then more time after that refinishing, recovering and generally refurbishing. Everything she owned, she'd earned, and it all meant something to her. "Oh?"

He slid a glance her way. "It's softer. Some reason I figured you more for acrylic and steel."

Her lips tightened. "Like my personality, I suppose?"

"I'll plead the fifth on that." He picked up a needlepoint pillow of pale yellow and blue. "Better never let Harvey see this place. It's got cupcake written all over it."

She huffed the hair out of her eye. "Great." If he was still angry, he was doing a masterful job of hiding it.

He cocked his head and studied her. "You look like you're headed for the gallows. What do you think I have planned?"

Now. Tell him now! She opened her mouth. "Nothing. I just need to—" A deafening burst of music from the apartment next door made her jump.

"Need to what?" He had to raise his voice over the racket.

She smiled weakly and gestured toward her shoes in answer. She quickly pushed her bare feet into her loafers and grabbed her jacket from the wrought iron coat tree next to the door. Whatever he had in mind had to be better than standing in her small apartment like this. "We should go." The door was still ajar and she pulled it wide. "It'll get louder before it stops."

Pax set the pillow back on her slipcovered couch and stepped past her into the hall. She locked up and shoved her key inside her pocket. The music was even louder in the hallway, where the walls seemed to vibrate.

"That go on a lot?"

She nervously headed for the stairwell, bypassing the elevator that was perpetually out of service. "Often enough. Fortunately, Gonzo's mom doesn't let him play it like that at night." She started down the steps. "Probably a different world than that fancy penthouse loft of yours."

Pax didn't bother denying it. He watched the thick knot of hair on top of her head bounce as she skipped down the stairs. "There was a cop car outside the entrance when I got here," he told her. And he hadn't breathed easy until he'd seen that the officers were focused on a unit on the second floor. Shea's apartment was on the third.

"The Boerners, most likely. He likes to drink and she likes to scream." She glanced back at him. "I'll take Gonzo's music over that any day of the week."

He had no clue what sort of salary she earned at the *Tub*, but it couldn't be much if this place was all she could afford. They reached the landing and started down the next flight. "Smells like onions here."

She glanced at him again and quickened her step. "Yeah. Sorry about that."

Her apartment, however, had smelled like vanilla and chocolate. The place had felt soft and feminine and inviting, and seeing it was proof that there *was* a soft, gooey center hidden inside her hard candy shell. "Reminds me of the first apartment I had after college."

They reached the next landing and she paused for a moment. "You went to Amsterdam after you finished college."

He didn't make the mistake of thinking she'd suddenly become curious. In her first interview with him, he'd told her about working with a boat builder there for nearly a year. "They have onions in Amsterdam, too."

She shook her head a little and began quickly descending the stairs again. Her feet pounded the steps rhythmically and he decided she'd had a lot of practice going up and down them. He was glad that he ran with Hooch every day, or he'd be puffing away like an old man trying to keep up with her.

"From what I understand," her voice echoed in the stairwell, "they have a lot of things in Amsterdam."

"You're a journalist, Shea. If you want to know something, you'd better learn how to ask it."

She shot him a skeptical look. "Legalized pot?"

He'd figured it would either be that or the sex shops in the Red Light District. It's what every tourist was curious about. "It wasn't legalized. It was just…low on the radar where the police were concerned." He waited a beat. "So I heard, anyway."

Her eyebrows rose. "You're saying you didn't partake?"

"I'm saying I never inhaled."

She absorbed that and suddenly laughed.

He could count on one hand the number of times he'd heard her laugh like that. Unfettered. Unselfconscious. It sounded good on her, and no matter how angry he'd been the night before, he knew he wanted to hear it more.

"So where are we heading, anyway?" she asked when they reached the dingy, minuscule lobby on the ground floor.

"Magnolia."

She visibly stiffened. "What's in Magnolia?"

"My grandparents live there."

She stopped walking altogether, giving him an alarmed look. "We're going to see your grandparents?"

He thought about warning her that they would be seeing a lot more people than just his grandparents, but he didn't. She'd probably turn tail and run, whether she needed quotes from him or not.

Phil had been right.

He needed to step up his tactics or Shea would keep him at arm's length until he was eighty.

"Yeah." He pushed open the door and tugged her out onto the sidewalk. It was uncommonly clear for the middle of February, the sky magnificently blue.

"*Why?*"

"Because they're expecting me," he said smoothly. And they were already late. He pointed at the SUV parked up the street. "Over there."

She looked from his face to the SUV and back again. "What happened to the cherry-red toy that costs more than I earn in a year?"

"It's taking the Sunday off, occupying the spot in my parking garage where this one usually lives." He pulled the key fob out of his pocket as they approached the SUV and the locks obediently chirped.

She was studying him as if he were a puzzle missing half its pieces. "You're always driving that car."

He opened the passenger door for her and refrained from grabbing her waist to help her inside. He didn't have quite so much control, though, when it came to appreciating the way her jeans fit her rear as she stretched her foot up to the high running board. "During the week," he agreed absently. Parking was easier to find with the Audi than with the SUV. "I'm thinking about selling the roadster anyway."

Maybe it was his partner's satisfaction with his newfound home life or maybe Pax was just getting older. Either way, his fast-lane lifestyle had worn thin. He wanted a house with a backyard for Hooch. And if he wanted speed, he could always take out *Honey Girl*.

He tried not to picture Shea in that backyard with him and his dog, but it was impossible.

She finally slid onto the seat and looked at him. "Already bored with it?"

"Is it habit for you to think the worst of everyone, or is that just with me?"

"I don't think the worst of you."

"Could've fooled me, sweetheart."

She swiped at the hair that kept falling down her cheek. "Well, clearly, I'm awful. So why do you bother with me at all?"

"Ordinarily, I'd ignore that. Because, once again, it's

nonsense. But since you're obviously in need of a remedial course in trusting people, I won't."

Color filled her cheeks. Probably from irritation, but at least she didn't look in danger of passing out.

"One." He reached out and tucked the silky lock of hair up into the long pin tenuously holding her mass of hair on top of her head. "I do not think you're awful. I think you're clever and smart and too jaded for your own good. And two—" He broke off.

Her eyes were wide. Waiting.

He stomped on the urge to kiss her. "And two...you're just going to have to wait for and realize for yourself."

He pushed her door closed, noting the confusion clouding her eyes, and walked around the SUV.

She kept saying that relationships didn't last?

It would be interesting to hear what she'd have to say when they arrived at his grandparents' seventy-fifth wedding anniversary.

Chapter Five

The number of cars parked along the tree-lined street was Shea's first clue. The enormous gold, silver and white balloon arch that soared high above the brick walkway leading to the front door sealed the deal.

She looked up at the bobbing balloons as they walked beneath them, trying not to panic. She grabbed Pax's arm, wanting to slow him down, and bumped right into him when he stopped. Her nerves fizzed even more and she quickly stepped back so that her breasts weren't pressed against his arm. "Want to give me some context here?"

"It's a party."

She hadn't felt like stomping her foot since she'd been twelve and her mother had told her that she was divorcing Ken. "I realize that!"

The smile that had been so noticeably missing the night before was back in his eyes, almost providing a soothing balm to her rising anxiety. "I had suspected, but I'm just now realizing what a control freak you really are."

She couldn't be bothered being offended when she knew good and well that he was right. "What *kind* of party?"

"It's my grandparents' anniversary."

She groaned. "Pax! I can't be going in there for something like that!"

"Because you're morally opposed to celebrating wedding anniversaries?"

She made a face. "Because it's a *family* thing."

"Yup. Lots and lots of family packed into a house too small to hold them all." He closed his hand around her arm and started toward the front door again, pulling her along whether she liked it or not. "Pretend it's an assignment and put a smile on your face. It's not a freakin' execution, for Pete's sake."

"But it's not an assignment. And no amount of pretending is going to make it feel like one."

"Couple hours, remember?" He pushed open the front door and pulled her inside the house.

She wasn't likely to forget.

The second they entered, it was as if they'd walked into the center of a circus.

Unlike her mother's oversized showplace, Pax's grandparents' home was modestly sized. And it was currently bulging at the seams. Little kids chased each other around batting balloons, big band music blared—not quite as loud as Gonzo's, but close—and through the sliding glass door that was opposite them, she could see adults standing around outside cheering at something.

"Pax!" Beatrice appeared in the living room, rounding a comfortably dated couch. "Hey there, Shea!" Gone was the brilliant red dress, but Pax's sister was just as striking now in a white T-shirt and colorful tie-dyed skirt as she had been the night before. "Hurry up." Beatrice opened the sliding glass door and beckoned. "Grammy and Granddad are out there swing dancing. It's a hoot!"

Pax's grip on her arm didn't lighten up as they threaded their way past the kids. Maybe he thought she'd cut and run if he didn't hold on to her, though she supposed she couldn't blame him if he did.

She sidestepped a little girl with lopsided blond pigtails and would have been happy to hover in the doorway behind Pax if he hadn't pulled her around in front of him and nudged her farther out onto what she realized was a wooden deck that seemed nearly double the size of the congested living room.

He closed his hands over her shoulders. "Can you see?"

Pretty much all she could see were the backs of the people in front of her. And all she could feel was the heat of Pax standing so close behind her.

It wasn't fair that along with everything else, she had to stave off a shiver from his proximity.

He was still waiting for an answer, and she shook her head, too dry-mouthed to speak.

"Yo, Donny." He tapped the man directly in front of her. "Make a hole, man. Not everyone's oversized like the Merricks."

Donny, who looked remarkably similar to Pax but with gray flecks in his brown hair, glanced back at them. His face creased in a smile and he grabbed Pax in a shoulder-bumping hug, squashing right over Shea. "Sorry."

He grinned at her and Pax with such good nature, she managed a fairly natural smile in return. And then, before she knew what was happening, both men were pushing her forward until she was in front of the crowd and had a clear view of an elderly couple cutting a dauntingly spry jig.

The two were surrounded on all sides by people who

were smiling and laughing and cheering them on, but before long, the woman—obviously Pax's grandmother—begged off, laughing and pressing a hand to the string of pearls at her neck.

Her tall, thin husband kept shuffling his feet, though. "Come on, baby," he beckoned to a slender, graying brunette who was wearing a white apron over her dress and holding a toddler in her arms. "Give your old pop a dance."

"Give yourself a rest before you have a heart attack," Pax's grandmother told him wryly. She patted her white hair and moved toward where Shea stood, giving her a friendly smile. "Hello, dear," she greeted and squeezed Shea's hand lightly. "You must be Pax's friend."

Inside, Shea felt like quivering gelatin. Pax had obviously warned them she was coming, and for some reason, it completely unnerved her. "Shea Weatherby," she said. "Happy anniversary, Mrs.—" She realized she didn't know if the woman was a Merrick or not, but it didn't matter because her attention had turned back to her husband. He'd begun dancing with the brunette who'd passed off the toddler to Beatrice.

"Call me Grammy," the white-haired woman instructed her. "Everyone does." She clapped her hands together over her generous bosom. "Doesn't matter how old I get, it still does something to me seeing Daddy dance with his daughter."

Shea kept smiling as her stomach suddenly hollowed. "They're lovely together," she managed.

She slid back a step and bumped into Pax, who'd somehow worked his way behind her again. "Excuse me." She darted around him, desperate to escape, and caught the quick frown on his face before she made it past Donny and two other men and into the living room again, where pandemonium was still reigning.

The little girl with the pigtails was closest.

"Do you know where the bathroom is?"

The girl's feet bounced on the carpet as she batted a balloon across the room. Then she pointed.

It was enough direction for Shea.

She bolted down the hallway, and the second doorway she passed was mercifully an unoccupied bathroom. She darted inside, shutting the door and flipping the lock, as if Pax were likely to come in after her.

Her heart was racing as she tore off her jacket, quickly turned on the water faucet above the pedestal sink and shoved her hands under the cold water as she fought the nausea roiling inside her. Weak tears squeezed from the corners of her eyes as she looked at herself in the mirror.

It was the reflection of a mad woman, and she looked away.

She cupped her hands under the water and splashed it on her face. Then did it again. And slowly, the nausea abated. Her stomach settled. Her pulse slowed.

And when she heard a soft tap on the door, she cringed.

"Shea?" It wasn't Pax's voice. It sounded like his sister. "Pax says he thinks you're not feeling well. Can I get you anything?"

"I'm fine," she lied thickly for the second time that day, and it was barely noon. She snatched one of the pretty little disposable guest towels stacked on a shelf next to the sink and mopped her face quickly. Then she adjusted the pin more firmly into her bun, grabbed her jacket from the floor and pulled open the door to Beatrice's concerned face. "I'm fine," she said again.

The other woman's eyebrows rose a little. "Honey, you don't look fine." She glanced up the hallway toward the living room, then grabbed Shea's hand and tugged her out of the bathroom and in the opposite direction.

"Beatrice—"

"Pax sees you looking this white and he's going to come unglued." She nudged Shea through the next doorway into a bedroom. "Sit there." She pushed Shea toward the brass bed.

Shea sat. She felt like an utter fool. "Beatrice—"

"I used to sleep over here when I was a girl," Beatrice mused. "Grammy hasn't changed a thing since then." She grabbed something from the dresser and turned toward Shea.

Blusher, she realized when the other woman stroked a soft brush across her cheeks.

"Coming back to live with them has definitely been a blast from the past," Beatrice went on, as if there were nothing unusual about the situation at all. "And it's convenient to be here rather than over in Port Orchard where our parents live, but I really look forward to finding my own place. Just waiting for some financial stuff to be resolved first."

Shea tilted her face up obediently when Beatrice tapped her chin. "What made you decide to come back to Seattle?"

"Seemed like a good idea." Beatrice straightened and cocked her head in a gesture eerily similar to Pax's. She clucked her tongue, gathered up more blush on the brush and swept it lightly again over Shea's cheeks. "After my fiancé dumped me for our twenty-two-year-old receptionist." She made a face. "Didn't much feel like being partners with him in our planning business after that." She studied Shea's face for a moment, then nodded and sat on the foot of the bed beside her. "Much better."

Shea looked at her with sympathy. "Been there. Bruce dumped me two days before our wedding."

Beatrice's response was immediate. "Crumb."

She didn't know why she found that amusing, but she did. "Yeah. He was definitely that."

Standing outside in the hallway, Pax slowly balled his hands into fists as he listened to Shea's low voice. He knew eavesdropping was rotten, but he couldn't make himself stop.

"How long ago did it happen?" he heard his sister ask.

"Not long enough." Shea's voice was soft. "Almost three years now. Supposed to be a big white June wedding and all of that. My mother was in wedding-planning heaven."

Pax exhaled and turned, leaning silently against the wall outside the bedroom door.

The regatta that Shea had been covering for the *Washtub* when he'd met her had been nearly three years ago. Over the Fourth of July holiday. The crumb had probably just jilted her.

"We'd picked a date in November," Beatrice was sharing. "Canceling the wedding plans turned out to be a lot easier than getting out of the business with him, though."

"I'm guessing that would be the financial stuff," Shea said.

"Mmm-hmm. How long were you engaged?"

Pax heard a footstep and he glared at Donny, who was sauntering down the hall toward the bathroom. His cousin lifted his hands peaceably and turned on his heel.

But the interruption was enough to jab Pax's conscience. He made a sound and stepped into the doorway.

Shea's eyes rounded, looking at him guiltily.

He couldn't blame her for confiding something in his sister that she'd never confided in him, but it still bugged the hell out of him. "How long *were* you engaged?"

Rather than shying away, though, her eyes narrowed.

"Didn't you ever learn that listening through keyholes wasn't polite?"

He put his hand pointedly on the open door. "Shut the door next time. Bea." He didn't look away from Shea. "Mom's looking for you."

Beatrice hesitated only briefly. "Sure." She hurried out of the room.

Pax pushed the door closed behind her. The house was small and packed with people. He wasn't going to chance anyone else overhearing. "You could have told me."

Shea pressed her lips together for a minute. "Whenever we've been together, the point hasn't been to talk about me. I've been working, and it's always about you. Or your partner. Or your latest pet project."

"You weren't interviewing me the night of the ice storm."

She looked away and pushed herself off the bed, rubbing her hands down the thighs of her jeans. "A-about that."

"Is that when you started believing that relationships never last?"

"When I slept with you, or when I was left at the altar?"

He looked at her and her flippant expression faded. She shook her head and rubbed the line forming between her eyebrows. "I learned that when I was a kid," she said abruptly. "Bruce was an incredibly stupid aberration."

"He was an ass."

Her gaze flicked to his. "Yes," she agreed after a moment. "I suppose he was. But my mistake was in forgetting what I already knew." She clasped her hands around her waist. "Relationships, and especially marriages, don't last."

"Really?" He jerked his head toward the door. "They're celebrating seventy-five years out there. My parents have been married for forty. Donny—my cousin—he's going on twenty, with his oldest kid graduating from high school this year and his youngest just starting kindergarten. All those kids playing in the living room? Pretty sure their parents—all cousins of mine, by the way—are believing in their marriages, too."

Her throat worked. "Congratulations." She spread her hands wide and paced away from him, putting the width of the bed between them. "*My* mother has been married seven times! I have more stepsiblings than Carter's got pills and none of *them* have managed to make a marriage work, either." Her eyes searched his. "You're thirty-eight and in the time I've known you, I've never seen you serious about anyone! If you're such a big believer, why haven't you taken the plunge?"

"Because when I do, there's no getting out of the water. Not for me."

She frowned at him. "Well. That water's not for me. I don't *swim*. You're not natural. You know that?"

He struggled not to lose his patience altogether. "Because I believe in having what my parents have? What my grandparents have? Because I'm smart enough to wait around until I have someone standing by my side who wants that, too?"

Her eyes flooded. "Well, I hope she's got an understanding nature," she said hoarsely.

His hair stood on end, and he suddenly had the feeling he was stepping through a minefield. "Why?"

"Because I'm pregnant!" The words whooshed out of her, seeming to echo around the room.

He was vaguely aware of the music and noise coming from the rest of the house where the party was going strong. But just then, the only thing he could hear was his pulse clanging inside his head.

She sank down on the side of the bed as if her legs had stopped functioning.

He wasn't sure his own legs still worked, when it came down to it. They'd gone numb.

"You're...pregnant," he repeated slowly. The words circled inside his head, along with his pulse. "Pregnant. As in...pregnant."

She nodded once, not looking at him.

"Since when?" On the stupidity scale of one to ten, a kernel of his brain realized that the question was about a seventy-two.

Her fingers kept plucking at the bedspread beneath her. "I just found out."

"When? Today? Is that why you were as skittish as a cat when I picked you up?"

"Friday," she whispered. "I took a home pregnancy test." Her jaw canted. "Or two." Her lashes lifted. "And don't jump on me for not telling you immediately," she sounded defensive. "I *tried*." She turned her palms upward. "And now I'm ruining your grandparents' party," she said thickly.

He heard her, but the words didn't really penetrate.

"We're having a baby." It was beginning to sink in. And something was tightening inside his chest.

Her eyes were wet, but she still managed to glare at him. "I just said so, didn't I? Don't worry. I don't expect anything from you."

It was easier to battle down the bolt of anger at that than it was the sting of pain. "Then you're a fool if you don't." He wasn't even aware of moving, but he must have. Because suddenly he was standing right in front of her, knees going out from beneath him as he knelt down. He put his hands on her hips, feeling the way she trembled. "It hasn't even been two months since the ice storm. You're really sure?"

"Eight weeks and three home pregnancy tests sure." She

sniffled. "I'm sorry, Pax. I never thought—" She broke off, looking shocked when he pressed his palms against her flat abdomen.

"Hey there, buddy." He cleared the knot from his throat. "Tell your mom if she says she's sorry again, I'm going to put her over my knee." He looked up at her. "We were *both* there, Shea."

Her nose was red and tears started crawling down her cheeks. "You're not even going to ask if it's yours?"

He managed not to swear, but it was close. "You wouldn't be this upset about telling me if he weren't." He wanted to brush away her tears and make her believe that everything would be fine. But he hadn't gotten to where he was in life by lying to himself. He knew he couldn't make her believe anything that she wasn't ready to believe.

Given the glut of personal information he'd learned about her in the past ten minutes—more than she'd ever shared in all the time he'd known her—he had to face the fact that there was no guarantee that she'd ever even get to that point of believing.

So he satisfied himself for now with addressing her belly again instead. "Mommy has a lot to learn about your old man," he murmured.

"You keep referring to the baby like it's a boy. You don't know that."

"Six generations of Merricks." He ignored the leaping inside his chest and straightened, pulling her to her feet. He could span her waist in his hands and her head didn't even reach his shoulders. An image of her, heavy with a baby, floated inside his head. Would their son be dark-haired like he was? Have Shea's blue eyes?

The knot was back in his throat. The backyard in his mind suddenly possessed a tire swing and a sandbox.

"First baby has always been a boy," he managed. "Second baby's always a girl."

Alarm filled her eyes. "Second! We're not having a second baby. We shouldn't be having a first!"

If she'd wanted to end her pregnancy, she would have done it. And she never would have told him. He knew that much about her. "But we *are*," he said steadily. Which was pretty damn impressive as far as he was concerned. It wasn't like he'd gotten up that morning suspecting this sort of news. "Have you told anyone else?"

A burst of laughter from the partygoers caused her to jerk, her breasts bumping into him. She hastily stepped back as far as the bed would allow and wrapped her arms around herself. "Who…like Harvey? He doesn't need to know I'm pregnant. Not yet anyway." Her soft lips twisted. "He'll probably stop sending me out on anything and assign me to coffee runs when he finds out."

"I meant your family, sweetheart." But he knew the answer now.

She sidled past him, giving him as wide a berth as space allowed, and paced around to the other side of the bed. "It's your baby. You deserved to be the first."

Which didn't say anything about her plans for telling her frequently married mother.

"I guess I should thank you for that."

Her gaze skidded over his and away. She rubbed her hands down her thighs and tucked her fingers in her back pockets. "Thanks for not suggesting that we should get married. Or…or anything ridiculous like that."

He let that slide for now. His brain had already been filled with plans, and none of them were ridiculous in his estimation. Particularly now. "Three different home tests? But you haven't seen a doctor."

"No. I told you. I just—"

"—found out. Right. Do you have someone in mind?"

"No."

"You're just taking things one step at a time, I guess."

Her lashes lifted. The corners of her soft lips rose in a forced smile. "Pretty much."

There was a tapping on the door. "Pax?" His mother's voice was soft but distinct. "Your grandparents are starting to open their gifts."

He didn't take his eyes off of Shea. She'd shifted restlessly at the knock, pulling her hands from her pockets to wipe her cheeks. He raised his voice. "Be there in a second, Mom."

Shea groaned softly. "I've crashed an anniversary party and didn't even bring a gift."

"You kidding? You've got the biggest damn gift of the day."

Her mouth rounded as his meaning obviously sank in. "What? No." She shook her head so hard that the lock of hair tumbled over her cheek again and was joined by a few more. "Oh, no. No, no, no." She leaned forward, pressing her palms flat against the mattress. "We are *not* telling them I'm pregnant."

"We're going to tell them sooner or later. Can't think of a better time than now." Leaning over the way she was caused the scooped neck of her pink T-shirt to gape, giving him a mouthwatering view of creamy skin barely contained by sheer lace.

She must have realized it because she straightened like she'd been jabbed in the spine with a hot poker. She yanked the hem of the shirt around her hips.

"Unless you figured on waiting until after he's born," he continued. "*No*," he added when he saw the glint appear in her eyes. "I'm not serious. That is not going to happen.

Maybe you don't want to tell your mother, but my entire family is here."

"And they're going to know exactly what happened!" As pale as she'd been earlier, her face was filling with color now.

"I wasn't planning to give them the exact details," he drawled.

"You know what I mean," she huffed. "They know we're not…not—" she made a face and waved her hands "—romantically involved."

They didn't know anything of the sort, but telling Shea that would only inflame her further. "Would you prefer that they thought we were?"

"No!" She flopped her hands at her sides and shook her head. "I don't know," she muttered. "My mother's always said to get a ring on your finger first. The only time I have a one-night stand, and look what happens."

"We've known each other more 'n two years, Shea. Not exactly a one-nighter in my book."

"Yeah, but we haven't…haven't dated or anything."

"And whose doing was that?" He didn't wait for an answer. "What do you think a date—" he air-quoted it "—or two would have changed anyway? You wouldn't have learned anything more about me over dinner or drinks or whatever constitutes a date in your mind than you already know. *You* are the one who's the mystery. Not me." He figured that was a debate she'd try to keep going indefinitely, so he stepped over to the door, pulling it open. "I told them you were my friend. That's all they need to know. Now come on."

"Pax—"

She looked truly miserable, and it gave him a pain in his gut. Dammit. "I have a gift certificate for them in the truck," he said gruffly. "I had Ruth set them up for a hot air balloon ride. They've always talked about it but have never done it."

"That's…that's so sweet."

It was his turn to grimace. "Yeah. *Sweet.* That's what every guy goes for."

"It's true, though." She chewed at her lip, slowly moving toward him and the door. She stopped when she reached him and looked up at him. "I don't know where we go from here," she whispered.

"That's okay." He slid the loose hair behind her ear and forced himself not to clasp her head in his hands and cover her mouth with his. "People have been having babies for a long time," he murmured. "We'll figure it out, too."

They both heard the audible gasp at the same time and turned to see his mom standing in the hallway, her hands clasped together in front of her white apron.

"Is it true?" she asked. "You're pregnant?"

Chapter Six

Shea's stomach dropped to her toes. She felt Pax's fingers squeeze her shoulder and he gave her an "oh well" sort of look that struck her as entirely too convenient.

"Yeah," he told his mom. "Shea and I are pregnant."

It was too much, hearing him phrase it that way. She couldn't even hold on to blaming him for spilling the beans, and her eyes stung with fresh tears all over again.

"Oh, my goodness!" Pax's mother looked teary herself. She hurried to them, reaching out to pull Pax into a hug. "I'd begun to think I was *never* going to get a grandchild!" She pushed him back only to tug his face down and give him a kiss. Just as quickly, she turned to Shea. "And Shea. We haven't even been properly introduced," she exclaimed, putting her arms around Shea, engulfing her in the soft scent of Chanel No. 5. "I'm Linda Merrick," the woman said, rocking back and forth excitedly. "Trust my son to keep his cards close to the vest." She pushed back enough to look up at Pax. "Can we look forward to wedding bells, too?"

Shea nearly choked.

"Mom." Pax's tone was warning, giving Shea the sense that the topic wasn't a new one. "Don't."

"Oh, fine," Linda said and turned her gaze back to Shea. She tightened her arm around Shea's shoulder. "This is what a mother gets for raising an independent cuss."

"Hon," a deep voice interrupted them, "your mother refuses to open another gift until you get back in there."

"Daniel." Pax's mother turned to look at the man who could only be Pax's father, the resemblance was so strong. She beckoned excitedly. "You're never going to believe it. Pax and Shea are having a baby!"

Pax's eyes met Shea's. "See? We don't even have to tell anyone. Mom'll do the heavy lifting."

Shea smiled weakly.

Pax's father didn't display quite the level of enthusiasm that his wife had, but his smile was pretty broad. He strode forward, giving Pax a slap on the shoulder while he looked at Shea. "We knew he was hiding someone special, but we had no idea it was this serious." He leaned over and kissed her on the cheek.

"Oh, now we're embarrassing her." Linda tsked. She let go of Shea, but only to grab her by the hand and squeeze. "Come on now." She pushed Pax's shoulder with her other hand, nudging him toward the living room. "Wedding or not, your grandparents are going to be over the moon when they hear." She grinned at Shea. "My husband's side of the family has been popping out grandchildren for years. But your baby will be the first great-grandchild on the Mahoney side."

Shea managed a smile. "Great."

"What about your family, honey? Are there many grandchildren yet?"

Shea thought about the wild assortment of people who'd moved in and out of her life. There were too many divorces to count, but she honestly couldn't say whether any of her one-time stepsiblings had produced any babies. Even if they had, they weren't remotely part of her or Gloria's lives. The only one to remain in contact with Shea's mother was Marco, and that was as her attorney.

She shook her head. "This is the first." And she could only imagine what Gloria would have to say about it. She certainly wouldn't be as happy as Pax's mother seemed to be.

"You know, the Merricks always have a boy first." Linda's eyes crinkled. "Might as well prepare yourself." They'd reached the living room, where the kids had stopped batting balloons around, but only because they'd been sent out onto the deck to make room for the adults, who were now crowded into every spare inch of space.

Shea plucked at the neck of her T-shirt, feeling way too warm.

"Everyone." Linda's voice rose above the voices. "Pax and Shea are pregnant!"

Her legs felt wobbly as she and Pax were sucked into the crowd as inexorably as quicksand. She was hugged, patted, squeezed and kissed, and though she recognized the display was well meant, it was still overwhelming. She preferred being an observer. Not a participant.

Pax was no help, either; he'd been drawn off to one side where a bunch of men of varying ages were slapping him on the back as if he'd just won the World Series.

"Give the girl some breathing room." Pax's grandmother finally tugged Shea down to sit on the edge of her chair with her. She was wearing a pair of half-glasses that she hadn't been wearing while she'd been cutting the rug with her husband, and she peered over the tops of them at Shea. "How far along are you?"

Shea swallowed. She knew to the day exactly how far. "A-about eight weeks."

Mrs. Mahoney nodded, looking pleased. "You and Paxton'll make beautiful babies together."

Babies? Shea could barely deal with the one. "I didn't intend for our news to take over your anniversary celebration, Mrs. Mahoney."

"Already told you, dear. It's Grammy." She patted Shea's knee. "Now, I know it's not fashionable to ask these things these days, but what are your plans? Is there a wedding in the wings or—"

"Don't bug her about that, Mom," Linda interrupted before Shea could stumble out some sort of reply. "I already tried. Pax and Shea are adults. I'm sure they know what they're doing."

Shea smiled weakly, wishing it were true. She could feel Pax's gaze from across the room. It was anybody's guess what *he* was thinking. Her stomach churned again and a bead of sweat crawled down her spine. She swallowed, then shifted uncomfortably.

"Who's your ob-gyn?"

Shea looked at the young woman who'd asked. Everyone had introduced themselves during the mad hug-fest. But though Shea was usually good with names, she was drawing a blank now. "I—" She swallowed hard again and dashed her hand over her damp forehead. She felt so closed in, it made her dizzy. "I don't have one yet, actually."

"Sara Montgomery is the one you want to see," the other woman said, earning several nods of agreement. "She delivered my three—"

"—and mine," someone added.

"—and I think she's the best ob-gyn in the city," the woman finished.

Jennifer. That was her name. She was one of Pax's cousins and the little girl with the lopsided pigtails was her daughter. For some reason, solving that particular mystery seemed to calm the nausea tugging at Shea's insides, though it didn't do anything for how overheated she felt.

"But she'll have a devil of a time getting in to see her," another mother was saying. "Last I checked, Dr. Montgomery's not taking on new patients."

Jennifer looked across at Pax. He was standing between his father and his grandfather. All three of them now had thin, unlit cigars clenched between their teeth. "You can get her in, can't you, Pax?"

Donny laughed, answering before Pax could. "Don't know about that. It's not like he can take the receptionist out for a sail to charm her into making an appointment. Those days are done, aren't they?"

Pax laughed, too, as his gaze found Shea's. She felt another bead of sweat creep down her spine. "I have better days in store now," he said.

The comment earned an "awww" from most of the women and wry laughter from most of the men.

Grammy patted Shea's knee. "Don't worry, dear. They won't light up those awful things in here. Maybe you should eat something. You're quite green around the gills."

Shea let out a soundless laugh that was short on humor and long on desperation. From where they were sitting, she could see the lavish buffet that was set out on the table in the dining room. "I don't think that's such a good idea right now, Mrs....Grammy."

The elderly woman smiled. "Dry cereal," she advised. "One of those sweetened types that parents hate and children love. Linda." She raised her voice to catch her daughter's attention. "Bring Shea some of that cereal we keep on hand for the children. She needs a little nibble to help settle her stomach."

"I know just the thing." Pax's mom hurried into the dining room, past the weighted-down table and through a swinging door that presumably led to the kitchen.

In the living room, the women started chattering about morning sickness and their methods for dealing with it, suggesting everything from pickle juice to acupuncture.

Shea wanted to sink through the floor.

She *hated* being the center of attention.

Pax had ditched the cigar somewhere and was working his way across the room to her. He crouched down beside the chair and looked up at her. "You're sweating."

"Thanks for pointing that out," she muttered.

He pressed his palm to her forehead and his brows pulled together. "Jesus. You're burning." He immediately rose and pulled her to her feet. "Come on."

"Pax—"

He leaned over to kiss his grandmother's cheek. "Tell Mom we're taking a rain check on the Cap'n Crunch. Shea's not feeling well enough. Love you." Then he tugged Shea around the coffee table and toward the front door.

"Pax, we can't leave like this," Shea said under her breath.

"Sure we can." He waved to everyone and pushed her out the door.

The cold air felt heavenly on her hot skin.

"It's rude!"

"You didn't want to come in the first place," he reminded her.

"Don't put leaving like this on me!"

He marched her along the brick walkway. "You have

a fever," he said flatly. "I'm taking you home and we're calling the doctor."

She wasn't sure she recognized him. The Pax she knew didn't go around giving orders and making demands, yet that's what he'd been doing since the night before at the fundraiser. "I don't have a doctor."

"Then we'll get you in to see that Montgomery lady."

"You heard them in there. She's not taking new patients. I don't need a doctor right now anyway. Just some aspirin or something and a nap." Preferably one not interrupted this time by dreams about *him* and his darned shirt!

He didn't bother responding. They'd reached the curb and he nudged her onto the low brick-topped retaining wall. "Sit there. I'll get the truck."

Simply being outdoors in the cold air where she could actually breathe without feeling hemmed in by people was making her feel better. "I can walk."

His hand on her shoulder kept her in place. "Sit."

She exhaled and spread her hands in a gesture of capitulation. "Fine." To prove she was staying put, she even crossed one leg over the other. "Satisfied?"

"I will be when you're not running a fever." He set off down the sidewalk. With all the cars parked on the street, they'd had to park a few blocks away.

Shea glanced back at the house when she heard footsteps. Bea was hurrying toward her, Shea's jacket in one hand and a sealed plastic bag in the other. "Here." She handed both to Shea. "The cereal," she explained when Shea peered at the contents of the bag.

"Oh. Thanks." She had no desire to put on her jacket, so she set it on the wall beside her. But she was admittedly curious as to what a few pieces of dry, sweetened cereal were going to do for her nausea. She'd always heard saltine crackers were the cure, yet that hadn't been one of the suggestions the women had batted around earlier.

Beatrice sat down, too. "My brother is crazy about you, you know."

Shea barely kept her jaw from dropping. She had absolutely no clue how to respond. Pax most definitely was *not* crazy about her. But they'd just announced, inadvertently or not, that she was pregnant with his baby. She didn't know much about how regular families functioned, but she was pretty sure they probably wanted some affection involved when there was a baby on the way.

"He'd skin me alive if he knew I was saying this," Beatrice continued. "I just…kind of felt like I needed to."

Shea gathered herself. "Why?"

"Because he's a good guy."

She could hear the sound of his truck coming up the street. "I know he is."

"He's not the kind of guy who'd do what your crumb or my crumb did."

Shea opened her mouth to say she knew that too, but she couldn't make the words come. In her experience, it didn't matter how decent a person started out being; when the relationship didn't work—and it never did—people sank to all sorts of new depths.

Beatrice sighed a little. "I guess I just wanted to say that I don't want to see him get hurt."

Shea frowned. "I'm not going to hurt Pax."

"You're holding all the cards, Shea. You're the one who's pregnant. *Do* you plan to marry him?"

She felt hot again. "He hasn't asked me," she said faintly.

"He will."

She pressed her fingertips into the bricks beneath her. If Pax suggested marriage, it would be only because of the baby. Marriages failed often enough without going into one because of convenience. And she couldn't imagine why he would suggest marriage anyway, when he'd already dismissed the idea to his own mother.

"Beatrice." She moistened her lips, trying to frame her words well. "I would never try to keep Pax from his own baby. He can be as involved as he wants to be."

The other woman gave her an incredulous look. "How can you be with Pax and have any doubt that he wouldn't *want* to be involved?"

Shea cringed. She'd always been better putting her words in writing. "I didn't mean to imply that. I'm just saying that I realize Pax has an equal say in this baby."

"Really?"

She nearly jumped out of her skin when Pax spoke. He'd double-parked the SUV on the street in front of her and was standing two feet away on the sidewalk.

She felt hemmed in by the intensity in his gaze on one side, and his sister sitting beside her on the other. It felt as claustrophobic as it had in his grandparents' living room.

"Really." She pushed off the retaining wall, dusted her hands and grabbed her jacket. She managed a smile for Pax's sister. "Thanks for the, uh—" She didn't know how to define Beatrice's unexpected "talk" with her brother standing within earshot. So she lifted the jacket. "For remembering my jacket."

Beatrice nodded. If she'd intended to say anything else, Pax didn't give her a chance because he took Shea's elbow and hustled her to the SUV, where he lifted her right off the ground and set her on the passenger seat.

She was so surprised, her heart just about shot out the top of her pounding head. But all he did was close the door, round the SUV and get in. "Seat belt," he reminded her.

She shivered, remembering the way he'd said the same thing the morning after the ice storm.

She fastened her seat belt and stared sightlessly out the window. She thought about how her mother's house was about five blocks away on a much larger lot with a waterfront view. She soon roused herself, though, as Pax drove out of the neighborhood. He clearly wasn't heading in the direction of her apartment. "Where are we going?"

"Dr. Montgomery is meeting us at the hospital."

She jerked around in her seat, nearly strangling herself on the seat belt, and impatiently dragged the strap away from her neck. "I don't need a darned hospital!"

"Probably not," he agreed. "But that's where she is this afternoon. She's going to fit you in."

She stared at him. "It didn't even take you ten minutes to get the car. How'd you arrange this so fast?"

His gaze slid her way. "The Hunt Foundation is a major donor for the hospital. I called Cornelia."

"I knew you begged coffee off her a lot, but I didn't realize you were on such familiar footing with her." She wasn't sure why it disturbed her so much to realize it. But it did.

"I called J.T. first," he allowed. "J. T. Hunt," he elaborated when she frowned at him. "One of Cornelia's stepsons."

"I know who he is." Pax and Eric often credited their meteoric success to a yacht they'd built for J.T. "I didn't know you were friends."

"What if we are? We've done a few builds for him now. He gave me Cornelia's personal number."

She actually *worked* for Cornelia, albeit part time, and she didn't know the woman's personal number. It was a simple matter of security, given the identity of her husband. Shea had never met the computer genius herself, though she'd once snagged a quote from Harrison Hunt's eldest son, Grayson, who now ran the mega-corporation his father had founded. But according to the rumors, Harrison was more than a little eccentric and highly protective of his wife.

"Fast work," she murmured. "Guess it proves that whole 'who you know' thing." Obviously, Pax was wealthy. He and his partner were extremely successful. But it was something else to think that he rubbed elbows with people like the Hunts. They occupied an entirely different stratosphere than regular mortals. "I suppose you had to go and tell Cornelia I'm pregnant, too."

"You think she wouldn't have noticed eventually?"

She groaned and pressed her head back against the seat. "She fancies herself a matchmaker, you know."

"Cornelia?" He laughed. "So what if she does?"

She just sighed and closed her eyes. Her head was throbbing worse than ever. When she felt Pax press his palm to her forehead again, she didn't even startle. She just wanted to grab his hand and hold it there—because his palm was wonderfully cool. Of course, she did no such thing, and after a second, his hand was gone.

For some reason, she wanted to cry.

"Why'd you take three pregnancy tests?"

She surreptitiously swiped a tear from her cheek. "I didn't trust the first two, obviously."

"Always with the trust thing."

She shot him a look only to find him smiling gently at her. Realizing he was just goading her because he could, she huffed and rolled her eyes. "Why were there so many relatives from your father's side at your maternal grandparents' party?"

"Because we're just one big happy family." He glanced at her. "My dad's folks would have been there too, but they're on a Mediterranean cruise."

"Fancy vacation," she murmured.

"One Gramps has saved his whole life to take his wife on."

"Why didn't you just send them, like you did with the hot air balloon deal?" She sounded cranky and didn't care. "You've got the money."

He smiled. "I would have but when you know them all better, you'll understand. Merricks and Mahoneys always pay their own way."

Even though she was burning up, she shivered, but she didn't know if it was fever or the thought of being around long enough to know the rest of his family that well.

A few minutes later, he pulled into the hospital parking lot. The sight of the medical complex sent anxiety shooting through her, but she pushed open her own door without waiting for him to do something mannerly like come around and lift her out of the truck the way he'd put her into it.

He locked the vehicle and joined her. "Decided you're in a hurry to see a doctor after all?"

"We're here," she said abruptly. Better that he think she was in a rush than figure out that she wanted to dissolve every time he put his hands on her. "Might as well get it over and done with."

"Let's do it then." He took her hand and led her toward the building.

Despite her earlier protests, Shea was relieved to discover they didn't have to go through the emergency department to see Dr. Montgomery. Instead, they went to an office on the fourth floor, where they could wait while the doctor was notified that they were there.

"I've always hated hospitals," she murmured when the volunteer who'd shown them to the office left and they were alone again. She got up from her chair and crossed to the room's sole window. It overlooked the parking lot and what seemed to be a sea of vehicles. "I remember getting my tonsils out when I was seven. I had to stay overnight and I was terrified being here all alone."

"Didn't they let your parents stay with you?"

"I suppose they would have if they'd have been interested or around." She rubbed her fingertips over the windowsill. "My parents had already split up by then. My father's been in Europe since I was a toddler."

"What about your mom?"

"Let's just say she's not overly endowed with maternal instincts." She turned and leaned back against the sill. The door to the office was closed, making the small space feel even smaller. Pax was sitting in one of the two chairs, his long legs stretched out in front of him, his hands loosely linked across his flat stomach. Considering he was the one who'd been so anxious to get her here, it annoyed the life out of her that he seemed so at ease, while she felt like ants were nibbling at her nerves.

"You said you had a lot of stepsiblings?"

She nodded. "How long do you think we're going to have to wait in here?"

He shrugged. "Who knows? It's not like this is a normal office visit." He pressed his hands to the metal armrests and pushed out of the chair. "Why do you always avoid talking about yourself?"

"It's hardly interesting," she muttered. She looked over her shoulder out the window and imagined that she could pick out Pax's SUV from her vantage point.

"I don't know about that," he mused. "I was interested to learn that you had your tonsils out when you were seven."

She looked back and found him closing the few feet of distance between them. Her mouth went dry. She couldn't back up any; she could already feel the cool windowpane against her spine. "There's nothing interesting about my tonsils," she whispered.

"Had mine out when I was seventeen. In this very hospital." He smiled faintly. "We might've been here at the same time."

She let out a disbelieving laugh. "The odds aren't very good that we were."

He tilted his head slightly, studying her face. He was so close that she could see just how densely brown his eyes were—not a single fleck of lighter color to be had. They were like melted chocolate. Smooth. Rich. Inviting.

"I don't have a problem with long shots," he murmured. "When Erik and I started the business, the odds were that we'd never succeed. But we did."

"Because you're good at what you do."

"Lots of people are good at what they do. Cornelia says you've got a gift for reading between the lines of all those letters and emails she gets. That you can sense the genuine article even before you start doing your digging. I find that fact about you very interesting."

"So you and Cornelia *have* talked about me."

He pressed his hands against the sill on either side of her and leaned down until his head was only inches from hers. Her breath stalled somewhere inside her chest. She dropped her gaze, only to find herself looking at his lips, which wasn't any safer.

"Some would consider," his voice seemed deeper than ever, "my chances with you to be a long shot. Yet…here we are."

"Because we got caught," she said hoarsely. "We had unprotected sex, and nature took advantage."

"Another interesting point. Why was it unprotected?"

His mouth was barely five inches from hers. She could barely breathe. "*I* haven't needed to be protected. Not since—" She broke off.

"Since…?"

She swallowed. "Since my fiancé dumped me," she admitted huskily. What was the point in pretending? He knew about Bruce now anyway. "What's *your* excuse? You've been the man of the town since before we met. Or don't you think a guy has any responsibility when it comes to safe sex? You figure it's a woman's duty to—"

"I had a condom in my wallet," he said gruffly. "And yeah. I know just by admitting it that you're going to figure I'm always on the make even though I'm not."

She swallowed. Her lips parted.

"But the point is, Shea." He leaned closer and his lips grazed hers so lightly she wondered fancifully if it was her imagination. "When I was with you, I couldn't think of anything *but* you."

"Sorry about the wait."

They both jumped at the intrusive sound of the door opening and the voice that accompanied it. Shea winced when her head thumped the window behind her, and she looked beyond Pax's wide chest to the doorway.

The doctor's bright eyes took them both in as she extended her hand toward Pax, who was closest to the door. "I'm Dr. Sara Montgomery," she greeted. "And I understand you two have a baby on the way."

Chapter Seven

It took another hour before Dr. Montgomery was finished examining Shea. She sent them home with a list of instructions and a starter pack of prenatal vitamins.

Not only had the comfortably middle-aged doctor officially confirmed what the home pregnancy tests had already revealed in triplicate, but she'd also confirmed that Shea had a sinus infection, which was causing the headache and the mild fever. She prescribed an antibiotic that was safe for her to take and wanted Shea to drink lots of liquids and rest for the next twenty-four hours.

She also wanted them to set another appointment to see her in her regular office in the next week or so.

Them.

Not just Shea.

The doctor believed they were a couple and had treated them accordingly.

They picked up the prescription at the hospital pharmacy and drove back to Shea's apartment in silence. She didn't know if Pax felt as shell-shocked as she did, and she was glad he didn't feel a need to bring up that near-kiss the doctor had walked in on.

Even though it had been hours since he'd picked her up, a police car was still parked in front of her building. And it had been joined by two others.

Pax studied the vehicles, clearly displeased by the sight. "Is there ever a time when a police car isn't parked outside your building?"

"There wasn't one here the morning after the ice storm when you dropped me off."

An aging van was just pulling out of a spot at the end of the block, and Pax hit the gas, sliding into the space before anyone else could get to it. "Every cop in the city was dealing with the storm," he countered. "Even the criminals were on ice. Wait here while I find out what's going on."

"Don't be silly." She started to push open her door but he reached right across her, grabbed the handle and yanked it shut again.

"I said, *wait*."

Her heart skittered around a little. "And if I don't want to *wait?*"

His arm was still stretched past her chest. His eyes met hers. The chocolate wasn't melted now. His gaze was hard. And determined. "Do you really want to test me right now, Shea?"

It galled her that she felt a shudder of excitement sliding down her spine. Her head still ached, she still kept breaking out in a sweat and he was still turning her on.

There was just no winning in her world.

"Fine," she said tightly. "I'll wait."

He didn't move immediately, though, as if he wasn't sure whether to believe her or not.

"You should move," she finally said, feeling a little desperate. "Wouldn't want you to catch my infection."

"Nice try. The doc said you weren't contagious." His gaze dropped briefly to her lips, but then he moved back. He pushed open his door and got out.

She watched him walk toward the building entrance and speak with the officers there. He was a head taller than both and looked a lot more physically fit.

She blew out a long, shaky breath. She was never going to be able to forget just how exquisitely fit.

After about five minutes, he headed back to the truck—his long stride making short work of it—and got back behind the wheel. "They're investigating a couple of break-ins." He looked at her. "You didn't mention that there had been a lot of them lately."

His voice was mild, but her nerves prickled warningly. "I didn't think it was worth mentioning."

"Has your apartment been broken into?"

She started to deny it but thought better of it. "Once. But it was last year, and the only thing worth taking was my television." She'd had her laptop with her at work when it had happened. She'd never left it at home again after that for the simple reason that she couldn't afford to replace it if it were stolen.

He didn't look particularly mollified, though. "You can't stay here."

She frowned, glancing toward the police officers. "Did they tell you that?"

"No. *I'm* telling you that."

She exhaled. "Well, like it or not, this is where I live."

"I don't like it." He was eyeing the police cars. "This is a crap area and you're pregnant."

Her hackles rose. "It's *my* neighborhood and there are at least a half dozen women living here who are pregnant."

She couldn't name names, but she'd certainly seen them. She'd unfastened her seat belt while she'd been waiting for him to talk to the officers, and now she pushed open the door, quickly sliding out before he could stop her. She grabbed the small bag with her prescription. "I'm going inside."

"Dammit, Shea—"

"My head is pounding and I want to lie down," she said flatly and shut the door on his annoyed expression.

Pax watched her stomp down the sidewalk toward the police officers. He couldn't very well toss her over his shoulder and drag her back to his place with them watching.

Stifling an oath, he pulled out his cell phone and called his sister. "I'm still with Shea," he said without preamble. "Can you go over and let out Hooch for a while and fill his dog bowl?"

Beatrice agreed readily. "Is she okay?"

"She's got a sinus infection, but she'll be fine. I'll talk to you later." She'd barely said okay when he ended the call.

He grabbed Shea's jacket that was sitting on the back seat along with the bag of dry cereal, locked the truck and headed after her, catching up with her in the building's stairwell.

She was climbing the steps with none of the energy she'd displayed earlier that day, and she gave him a resigned look. "Now what?"

"When's the last time the elevator worked?"

She huffed and turned to face the ascent again. "I don't know. Last year at some point, I guess."

"The elevators always work in my building."

"Hurray for you." She took a few more steps, and he could see the way she used the handrail to help pull herself up.

"You're supposed to be getting rest right now—not climbing three damn flights of stairs."

She lifted her hand. "Such is life." When she reached the first floor landing and stopped to take an audible breath, he'd had enough.

"This is stupid," he muttered, stopping her progress with one hand on her shoulder. He shoved the jacket he was carrying into her hands and slid his other arm under her legs. She tipped easily back into his arms and he lifted her up.

"What are you *doing?*" Her screech echoed through the stairwell.

"Just what it looks like." He built custom sailing yachts. By hand. It wasn't lightweight work, and she definitely was. Cradling her in his arms like a baby, he turned slightly so her feet wouldn't scrape the block walls of the stairwell and began climbing. "Might help if you'd put your arm around my shoulder," he suggested mildly. She was holding herself as stiff as a board. But heat was still radiating from her.

She slowly slid her right arm around his shoulder. "This is completely unnecessary."

"I guess so if you wanted to spend the next hour climbing the stairs. Because at the rate you were going, that's about how long it would take." He gave her a little toss, adjusting his grip under her knees and probably enjoying the surprised gasp she let out more than he should.

"This is mortifying," she mumbled. "I'm too heavy for this."

He laughed outright at that. She was curvaceous as hell, but she was still small. "If you weigh more 'n one-ten, I'll eat my hat."

"You're not wearing a hat." She sounded even grumpier, which made him want to smile.

"Would I need to eat it if I were?"

"It's not polite to ask a woman what she weighs."

He stopped mid-step. Jiggled her once as if he were testing grapefruit at a store. "Standing by the one-ten," he said and started up the steps again. "Maybe a pound or two less." He wished it were a pound or two more. Carrying her the way he was, he could feel the points of her hips and the ridges in her spine even more prominently than he had when they'd slept together. "You're pregnant. You should be gaining weight. Not losing it."

"Like I need reminding."

Her head bumped against his chest as he turned on the next landing and started up to the third floor. They were halfway up before she finally spoke again.

"They've really all been boys?"

"First baby? Yup. So don't bother thinking about any pretty little girl names. Be a total waste of time."

"Where'd your parents come up with the name Paxton?"

"Some great-great something on my mom's side had the last name of Paxton. For whatever reason, my folks liked it."

"You don't?"

He snorted softly. Only a few more steps now, and he was glad. Not because he was tired from carrying her—though a few flights of stairs with a woman in your arms was a workout, no matter how little she weighed—but because holding her this way was having a predictable effect. "When I was young, the other kids were tough on unusual names. I was Pox as often as I was Pax."

"*Pox?*"

"I was in the third grade and had a case of chicken pox."

She covered her mouth to muffle her laugh.

"Popped Erik in the mouth one time and we both got suspended." He grinned at the memory. "He never called me Pox again, though." They'd reached the top of the stairs and he stopped. "Push open the door, would you?"

She obediently leaned over and pushed on the bar and they stepped through the doorway.

The music that had vibrated through the hallway when they'd left earlier was now silent, but he could still hear sounds coming from each of the apartments as he carried Shea to her door and set her back on her feet. She unlocked the door with the key she fished out of her front jeans pocket, and he followed her inside.

Even though he'd already had a brief preview, the interior of the place was still a surprise to him. It was so feminine.

Not that Shea wasn't wholly feminine. She just wasn't girly about it. And while he wouldn't call her apartment girly, it was close.

He almost felt like a bull in a china shop.

The second she walked in, she dumped her pharmacy bag and jacket on the trunk in front of her couch and headed straight for the cat perch by the window, where she stroked her hand over the cat curled on top of it. "How's Marsha-Marsha?" he heard her croon.

He closed the door and moved her jacket to the coat tree by the door. "Where'd you come up with a name like that?"

She picked the cat up off the perch and gave Pax a shocked look. "Didn't you ever watch *Brady Bunch* reruns when you were a kid?"

"I guess I saw a few," he allowed. "I never watched much television."

She sat on the arm of the couch, cradling the cat to her chest. Even from where he was standing near the door, he could hear the cat's motor running. "What did you do?"

"Sports." She didn't have a lot of furniture. Just the couch, the trunk and an old metal thing situated against the opposite wall, holding a small television on top. The kitchen opened right onto the living area, and he assumed the bedroom and bathroom were along the short hallway opposite the apartment door.

She didn't invite him to, but he moved around the trunk and sat down on the opposite side of the couch. "When I wasn't playing on some team, I was sailing. I still don't get the Marsha-Marsha reference."

She slid from the arm onto the couch cushion, still holding the cat. "The show was about a blended family. Three boys, three girls. Marsha, Jan and Cindy."

"Right. I know that, at least."

"Okay. So, one episode, Jan was jealous of her perfect older sister." She pulled the pin out of her hair and tossed it on the trunk. Her golden hair slowly unfurled, sliding in a coil over one shoulder. "Marsha-Marsha-Marsha," she sing-songed. Then she made a face and suddenly leaned over to set the cat on the ground, but he saw the way her cheeks had gone red. "You had to be there, I guess," she muttered.

"Was that your favorite show?"

"Mmm-hmm." She pushed her fingertips through her hair, flipping it the rest of the way loose from the coil. "An idealized view of the perfect family." Her lips twisted. "Then I finally realized there was no such thing." She closed her eyes, still rubbing her head.

"You need to be in bed."

"Probably," she agreed on a sigh. "But you're sitting on it."

He got up so fast he bumped his shin on the trunk. She opened her eyes and looked at him curiously.

She had an infection. And he needed a cold shower. "Folds out?"

She nodded, but she'd already kicked off her loafers

and was stretching out on the couch. It wasn't anywhere near long enough to accommodate him, but she was able to lie full length on it with no problem. "Too much work right now."

"Don't you want a pillow or something?"

"It's in the hall closet."

He retrieved it, noticing that the hall closet also doubled as her clothes closet. He grabbed the pillow from the top shelf, carried it back to the couch and tucked it under her head.

She sighed and lowered her lashes as she settled her cheek on the soft fabric. "Thanks."

He reached out to move her hair away from her cheek but caught himself. He curled his fingers into a fist and moved away from the couch, going around the short breakfast bar, which was the only thing separating the kitchen from the living area. She'd taken one dose of her antibiotic when they'd left the pharmacy. But the doctor had also told her she needed to drink plenty of fruit juice or water.

One look inside her refrigerator told him that she had no juice. And nothing else either. Unless he counted tins of canned cat food, the shelves in her fridge were even emptier than the ones in his.

She only had three cupboards. One contained pots and pans. The next held at least a dozen cookbooks that had him stopping in surprise. It didn't matter to him whether she cooked or not, but the fact that he didn't know at all was just another reminder of how much about her was still a mystery. He pulled open the last cupboard to reveal a few glasses and a set of plates and bowls.

If she ever had company over for a meal, he was guessing she went the disposable cups and plates route.

He grabbed one of the glasses and filled it with water, then took it over to her.

Her lips were parted, her breathing slow and deep.

He silently sat down on the trunk, absently drinking the water that he'd gotten for her, and watched her sleep. She didn't stir even when he let himself finally reach over and slide his fingers under the silky hair falling over her face.

He gently tucked it behind her ear.

The cat jumped up onto the back of the couch, giving him a wary look from her slanted green eyes, before delicately stepping down onto Shea's side and arranging herself there.

Shea didn't even budge.

She'd told him the cat was sixteen years old. He imagined she was well used to the cat sleeping on her by now.

The feline settled her chin on her paws, but her eyes didn't shift away from his face. "You her protector, Marsha-Marsha?"

The cat's ear swiveled at the sound of her name. He could hear her purring, but the second he reached out to rub his finger over her small, calico-colored head, the rumbling stopped.

He lowered his hand, studying the cat and the woman for a long while.

When it seemed clear that Shea wasn't going to wake anytime soon, or that Marsha-Marsha wasn't going to sleep as long as he was there, he refilled the glass with water and left it within Shea's easy reach on top of the trunk. Then, just because it was time for Hooch to be fed and he figured Marsha-Marsha should be too, he uncovered the opened can of cat food that had been in the fridge and dumped the contents out into the empty dish sitting on the floor in the corner of the kitchen. The other dish next to it was still full of water.

He'd seen a folded blanket in the closet along with the pillow, and even though Shea had been too hot all afternoon, he got it down and unfolded it near her bare feet. Just in case.

Then he took the key that she'd dropped into a dish by the cat tree and let himself out of the apartment, locking it behind him.

He gave up the parking spot and drove around until he found a grocery store and stocked up on everything he could think of. When he returned to Shea's place, he ended up having to carry everything two blocks because that was the closest he was able to park.

At least the cops were gone, but that was the only positive note. By the time he'd hauled everything he'd bought up the stairs, he was ready to personally pay to have the damned elevator fixed.

When he finally reached her door, he had to set one armload of groceries on the floor so he could unlock it. He'd just slid the key into the lock when he spotted the kid watching him from the apartment next door. He nodded at him. "Hey."

The kid looked about ten and his eyes were narrowed suspiciously. "What's wrong with Shea?"

She hadn't wanted him to tell his own family about her pregnancy, so he doubted she'd want him to tell her neighbors. "Nothing."

"Then why're *you* here? Shea don't have people visit her."

Interesting to note. "She does today." He finished unlocking the door and picked up the grocery bags. "I'm Pax, by the way."

"I know. You're the boat guy."

Pax hesitated. "How do you know that?"

The kid's lip curled. "My ma makes me read Shea's paper. I seen your picture."

"Good for your mom." He hesitated, looking at the kid again. "You like sailing?"

"I dunno. Never been."

Which was a crying shame, as far as Pax was concerned, for anyone who lived near water deep enough to bear a boat. "Can you swim?"

The kid shrugged as if he couldn't care less. "Nah." He turned sideways and disappeared through his doorway.

Shea had admitted once that she didn't swim. Used it as an excuse whenever he'd invited her to go sailing with him. Both things he intended to change. If she'd just give a little.

He opened her door and went inside.

She hadn't moved an inch. She was still sound asleep, with the cat stretched out on top of her.

He quietly put away the groceries as best as he could and left what wouldn't fit in the cupboards on the counter next to the narrow stove. Then he made himself a sandwich from the provisions he'd bought, filled a glass with water for himself and sat on the hard, wooden stool at the breakfast counter to eat while he checked his cell phone and answered a bunch of emails from work.

He was watching the local news with the sound turned off and the closed captioning turned on when the cat suddenly leaped off Shea and returned to the perch. A second later, Shea stretched and sat up. Her bleary eyes found him sitting on the floor in front of the couch and she rubbed them, as if expecting him to disappear. "Why are you still here?"

"Not going to leave you alone. Not sick. And not here."

Her lips compressed, but all she did was swing her feet to the floor and push herself off the couch. She walked around it and stopped short. "You bought groceries."

No point in denying the obvious. He looked over his shoulder at her. "If you're hungry I'll make you a sandwich."

She lifted her hand to her head and looked at him. "You can't stay here."

"It's after eleven. I've been with you for more 'n twelve hours and you haven't eaten one thing. If you don't want a sandwich, I bought fruit and soup and a bunch of other stuff."

"There's no *room* for you!"

More stating the obvious. He'd had to push the trunk off to one side just so he'd have room to sit on the freaking floor. He'd had more room in the tiny place he'd rented in Amsterdam than Shea had in her studio apartment. "Then we'll pull out the bed." He pushed to his feet, managing not to wince at how stiff he'd gotten sitting on the floor. He stepped past her into the kitchen, grabbed the loaf of bread he'd bought and started unwrapping it.

She threw up her hands and stomped down the short hall. He heard her slam the bathroom door closed.

He continued making the sliced turkey sandwich, and it was sitting on a paper towel when she returned a few minutes later. She pulled out the wooden stool and sat down in front of the food.

"There's tomato and lettuce if you want it."

Her lips pressed together. She shook her head and picked up one half of the sandwich. He'd cut it in two for Shea, only because it was the way his mom always served it.

She took a slow bite then set it down again. He nudged a glass of water toward her.

"Surprised you're not insisting on milk," she murmured.

"The doc said juices and water for now." He reached over and felt her forehead. "Still warm." But not burning like it had been earlier. "Still have a headache?"

She chewed on her lip and shook her head. Then her shoulders rose and fell with a huge sigh as if she'd come to some decision. "Pax." She folded her hands together on the counter and looked up at him. The sleepiness had cleared from her blue eyes, and now they were just determined. "I—"

"No."

She frowned. "You don't even know what I'm going to say."

"And I know my answer is no." He picked up the sandwich and held it in front of her mouth. "Unless you're in danger of yakking this up, take a bite."

"That's disgusting." But she still grabbed the sandwich out of his hand, took a bite and set it back on the paper towel. She chased it down with a gulp of water. "I appreciate the sandwich, but—"

He leaned on the counter. "*No.*"

She gave him an annoyed look. Her lashes lowered for a moment, and when they lifted again, she gave him a saccharine-sweet smile. "Let's get naked and have hot, crazy sex."

He knew she didn't mean it but his body still leapt eagerly. "Yes."

She huffed, rolled her eyes and turned her back on him. But she'd grabbed the sandwich first. "Is this what you're going to be like for the next seven months?"

He smiled at the back of her head. "It is if you're going to insist on staying in this crapshack for the next seven months."

She shot him an offended look over her shoulder. "Don't call my apartment that."

"I'm calling the building that, not your apartment."

Mollified, she took another bite of the sandwich and looked away again.

He eyed the back of her tangled hair. It had looked the same way the morning after the ice storm. He'd wanted to wind his fingers in it then, and he wanted to do it now.

He deliberately relaxed his hands. "You've got a real

storage problem, though, considering you need to stuff half your clothes inside that trunk."

"I don't—" She broke off and hopped off from the stool. She turned and set the bread crust, which was all that was left from the sandwich, on the paper towel. She wiped her fingers carefully on the edge of the paper. "What's your point, Pax? You want me to move to a better neighborhood?" Her lips curved with sarcasm. "One more in keeping with the standards of someone like you, who keeps J. T. Hunt on his speed dial?" She stretched out her arms, encompassing the apartment around them. "I'm not changing who I am just because I'm pregnant with your baby! You're all interested right now about this, but I'm not going to change my whole life just because you say so."

He looked past her shoulder to the images on the silent television screen, letting his sudden anger tick down to a manageable level.

Only when he thought it was under control did he focus on her again. Her lips were parted, her chest moving with her harsh breaths. "Your life has already changed. *Right now,*" he emphasized quietly. "You. Are. Pregnant." His fingers dug into the cheap laminate countertop between them. "By definition, that means a baby *is* going to arrive. *Our* baby. Our son."

Her gaze flickered. Her nose reddened.

The level wasn't so manageable after all.

He wanted to shake her. He wanted to kiss her.

And he was damned close to doing both.

He rounded the breakfast bar, hearing the almost-silent way she sucked in her breath. He pushed her chin up with his thumb until her wide eyes met his.

"Change is already here, sweetheart. And the sooner you accept that, the better," he finally said. Then he let go of her, and he walked out of her apartment.

Chapter Eight

Shea sat across the desk from Cornelia Hunt in the woman's elegant office and tried to keep her mind on what she was saying rather than letting it drift to the brick building next door.

Since Pax had walked out of her apartment two days ago, she hadn't heard one word from him.

"—disappointed, of course. You're really certain?"

She belatedly tuned back into Cornelia, realized she'd completely missed what the other woman had just said and wanted to kick herself. She couldn't afford to lose this job. Especially after Harvey had blown a fuse when she'd turned in her story about the charity auction and it had been missing his one required element—a heavy dose of Paxton Merrick. Unfortunately, with no time to resolve that before they went to press, he'd yanked the article altogether, which just left Shea feeling worse than ever because Beatrice had done a lot of work and Fresh Grounds deserved better.

"I'm sorry," she said now, looking at Cornelia. "What did you say?"

Cornelia folded her hands together on top of her spotless off-white desktop and the gigantic pink diamond on her wedding finger winked in the light from one of the crystal sconces on the wall. Her softly lined face creased in a kind smile. "Why don't you tell me what's bothering you, Shea?"

She wanted to squirm in her chair like a child caught out by her favorite teacher. Since she'd arrived that afternoon to pick up her latest assignment from the woman, she'd been waiting for Cornelia to say something about Pax asking her to intercede with the hospital and Dr. Montgomery's supposedly full patient load. To say that she knew Shea was pregnant.

But she hadn't.

Which left Shea realizing that Pax hadn't spilled the beans to Cornelia after all.

"Nothing," she insisted. "I…I just know you're disappointed about Elise Williams. I know she said her ex-husband was the one to incur those gambling debts, but that'd be tough when she's never been married at all." The woman had misrepresented a lot more than that, which Shea had also included in her report.

Cornelia made a soft "mmm" sound and turned slightly to rise from her desk. She crossed the spacious office, passing the set of imported loveseats situated in the center of the room and stopping in the corner, where windows looked out over the marina in one direction and Pax's building in the other.

Her silver-blond hair was smoothed back in its usual twist, but with the sunlight low on the horizon behind her she seemed to glow a little as she stood at the windows. She was old enough to be Gloria's mother, but as much effort as Shea's mother put into remaining ageless, she'd never achieve what Cornelia exuded so naturally. "Phil is more disappointed about Elise than I am. She believed the woman's story and it's never nice to know you've been lied to. Which is why we have *you*." Cornelia poured herself a fresh cup of coffee and glanced at Shea to see if she wanted some.

"No, thank you." Among other things, Dr. Montgomery advised her new obstetric patients to limit their caffeine intake, and she'd already had a small coffee that morning. It was tough, though, particularly when Cornelia carried her cup—delicate-looking china complete with saucer—back to the desk and the rich scent of Seattle's Best reached her.

She realized she was chewing the inside of her cheek and made herself stop. "Were there any letters that you wanted me to vet this week?" Ordinarily, Cornelia had a file ready and waiting for her.

"Oh, yes." The woman dismissed the notion that there might not be with a wave of her fingertips. "But I wondered if you'd consider a little extra duty."

Shea sat up a little straighter. A smart person didn't turn down a request from someone like Cornelia Hunt. Especially when there was a chance that Shea might be fired soon by her ornery editor. "What do you have in mind?"

"Up until now, I've given *you* the specific Cindys that needed vetting. The projects that we decided looked promising." Cornelia moved her cup and saucer a few inches to the side and opened a drawer in her desk to withdraw a bulging, oversized manila envelope. She set it on the desktop and slid it toward Shea. "I'd like you to read through these letters for me."

In addition to Phil, Cornelia already employed a half

dozen other people to deal with the constant stream of business proposals and outright pleas for handouts they received at FGI. Shea couldn't imagine why Cornelia was giving her these. "Am I looking for something in particular?"

Cornelia's smiled slightly. "Our next Cinderella project, of course."

Shea immediately pulled her hand back from the fat envelope. "I'm not qualified for that."

Cornelia eyed her thoughtfully. "Do you remember when you brought me the first batch of mail that had been sent to me in care of your newspaper?"

Shea wasn't likely to forget. Even though she'd miraculously gained an interview with Cornelia after that fashion show of Joanna Spinelli's, she'd had to jump through more than a few hoops to meet with her again in order to hand over the insane quantity of communications they'd received for her.

"I pulled out a random envelope to glance through and then I asked you what your opinion was," Cornelia continued.

Shea remembered very well. "I told you the woman was either greatly exaggerating or lying outright."

Cornelia nodded. She sat forward. "I had my son-in-law, Max, do what you do now. He looked into her story for me."

Shea frowned. "You didn't tell me that before."

"I wanted an impartial opinion. Max's company has an entire department that does this very thing." She opened another drawer in her desk and withdrew an opened envelope. "This is the letter. Not only did Max confirm your instinctive assessment, but he also wanted me to give him your name so he could offer you a job himself." She smiled slightly, dropping the thin envelope back in her drawer and closing it with a soft snap. "I love Max dearly, but I wasn't about to let him steal you right out from under my nose. I've always had this in mind, Shea."

She nudged the package toward her again. "At least give it a try. I know you have responsibilities at the *Washtub,* so I'm sending you home with this small batch to read at your convenience over the next several weeks. If anything here gives you a little tingle," her eyes smiled, "then set the letter aside so we can discuss it further."

She lifted her hand, forestalling Shea's objections. "And if you're worried that I don't intend to keep you on the payroll doing the investigations that you've been doing, don't." She sat back in her chair once again. "Selfishly, I wish we didn't have to share you with Harvey Hightower. You write beautiful articles, but I happen to think you could do quite a lot right here."

Shea couldn't do anything but stare. "I appreciate the confidence, Cornelia, but I'm not a—" she made herself say it "—fairy godmother."

Cornelia's calm expression didn't change. "I know you don't care for the term. But what is it that you think it means?"

Feeling even more on the spot, Shea shifted in her chair. "I think what you're doing to empower women in business is wonderful," she said carefully. "Particularly because you choose individuals who've legitimately had a rough time of it."

"I sense a but."

"But I've heard what happens with the women you help."

Cornelia's eyebrows rose a few millimeters.

Shea wished she'd just kept her mouth shut, but she was in the soup now. "How they all seem to end up finding—"

She broke off and shifted again. "Well, finding romance along the way."

"Not all of them. It's certainly not what I'm trying to accomplish here." Cornelia smiled a little. "But if they do, I simply consider it a happy coincidence." She nudged the envelope another inch and her entirely nonthreatening smile widened. She was merely a gracious older woman making a seemingly simple request. "Now, will you at least give it a try?"

Shea knew she couldn't possibly refuse. Not just because Cornelia was a Hunt, but because the woman *was* genuinely nice. She reluctantly set the envelope on her lap, trying not to sigh.

"Wonderful." Cornelia rose again, carried her coffee cup back to the table and glanced out at the view. "Now there's a sight." She nodded toward the marina-side windows. "Every time I see that delightful boy's yacht it takes my breath away."

Shea's stomach tightened, but she could no more prevent herself from getting up and going over to the window than she could stop herself from breathing.

As far as she was concerned, Pax was far from a delightful *boy,* but his sloop, *Honey Girl,* was instantly recognizable as it slowly pulled into the marina. From their vantage point on the second floor, she couldn't quite see him aboard, but she felt sure there wouldn't be anyone else piloting the yacht. He'd told her once that Erik was the only other person he trusted at the helm. "It is beautiful," she murmured.

"Has he taken you out on her?"

A pang shot through her. "No." Not because he hadn't offered. She'd just always turned him down.

"My daughters and I went out with J.T. years ago on the first sailboat Pax and Erik did for him and it was—" her eyes seemed lost in the memory "—just unforgettable." She focused again on Shea and patted her shoulder. "You should ask Pax to take you out on her. You won't regret it."

Shea had plenty of regrets, not the least of which was the way things had ended so horribly at her apartment.

Cornelia was waiting for some sort of response, so Shea gave her a noncommittal smile. "We'll see." She hugged the fat envelope she was still holding to her chest and returned to the chair where she'd left her purse. "I'll read the letters as soon as I can," she promised.

"I know you will." Cornelia started to follow her out of the office but stopped when her telephone rang. "I'd better get that," she said. "Harry's the only one who calls on that line. I'll see you on Friday."

Shea nodded and left the office, working her way around the scaffolding that seemed to find a new position every time she visited. The workers were long gone for the day, as were the rest of Cornelia's employees, and when she reached the bottom of the curving stairs, her footsteps echoed on the marble floor.

She hesitated, glancing in the direction of the kitchen where Pax always seemed to be hanging out whenever she came by, slugging down coffee like it was water and filching a chocolate if there happened to be any around. But he hadn't been there today and she knew it wasn't coincidence.

He'd accused her often enough of avoiding him, but now he was the one avoiding her.

The knowledge sat like a hard stone in the pit of her stomach as she left the building and crossed the quiet street toward her car parked on the other side. She opened the trunk and tossed the envelope and her purse inside.

Then, before she thought better of it, she slammed it shut and quickly retraced her steps, aiming for the paved breezeway between his building and Cornelia's. The strong breeze off the bay hit her, and she ducked her head against it, turning onto the walkway that ran behind the buildings. She could see *Honey Girl*'s distinctively tall mast several piers down, and she headed through the unlocked gate that blocked off the marina from the walkway.

Instinct was the only thing propelling her forward because she had no clue what she intended to say to him once she reached him. She just knew that she had to do— say—something.

Walking faster, nearly skipping, she clutched the lapels of her blazer together with one hand and caught her blowing hair in the other as she made her way along the dock. Her heart felt like it had transplanted itself in her throat by the time she turned and headed down the narrower, bobbing pier, just in time to see Pax leaping easily from his sailboat with a thick white rope in his hand. He was wearing jeans and a black weatherproof jacket, but his head was bare and his thick brown hair ruffled in the breeze.

Everything inside her went warm just looking at him.

She knew when he spotted her because he went still for a moment before he crouched down and rapidly tied off the rope. Then he pulled a ramp around, deftly flipped it out toward the side of his boat and re-boarded. He headed toward the back, where he smoothly jumped to the pier once more with another rope in hand.

The knots in her stomach rivaled the knots he was making around the huge cleats on the pier. She swallowed and started forward again. But she stopped dead when she heard the peal of a woman's laughter coming from the sailboat.

A redhead was picking her way around the riggings toward the ramp that Pax had put in place.

Shea's hands fisted as she watched him hold out his

hand with an easy smile to help the woman safely across to
the pier. Shea instinctively took a step back. Spun around
to leave. But the memory of his expression the night of the
fundraiser swam inside her head, bobbing as insistently
as the water sloshing against the pier.

She made herself stop. And slowly turn back.

The woman was on the pier now, her head thrown back,
her red hair streaming behind her in the breeze as she
looked up at Pax. If Harvey ever knew about the gloriously
perfect picture they made and how Shea didn't even try to
catch it on film, he'd can her for sure.

She could hear their voices, but the wind stole the
words. Unable to bear watching, she let go of her own
hair and let it blow across her eyes. Concentrating on the
faint motion of the pier beneath her feet was better than
counting the seconds inside her head, waiting for…some-
thing, even though it made her vaguely dizzy.

Finally, she heard footsteps and she looked up to find
the redhead approaching, her gaze curious as she passed
Shea. "Wind out here's hard on the hair, isn't it," she com-
mented brightly.

"Little bit," she agreed tightly.

"Worth it, though. Can't wait until the next time." The
woman smiled brilliantly and sent Pax an exuberant wave
before continuing on.

It was unkind of Shea to wish she would slip and land in
the drink, but she couldn't help giving it a passing thought.
Then she saw Pax heading toward her. She impatiently
raked her hair back from her face and waited.

He stopped a foot away from her and pushed his hands
into the pockets of his jacket. His expression was unread-
able. "Feeling better?"

She had been, until she'd seen him with the redhead.
"Yes. You've been out sailing." *So says the master of the*

obvious. She mentally kicked the mocking voice inside her head to the curb.

"Prospective client," he said.

If her jaw clenched any tighter, her molars were going to need dental attention. "For what? Private sailing lessons?"

He looked at her for a moment, then shook his head. He strode back to the boat, crossed the ramp in a single step and jumped back onto the deck.

Her insides squeezed. It hadn't been annoyance in his eyes but disappointment.

She went after him, stopping shy of the ramp. "I'm sorry."

With a life jacket in his hand, he straightened and then ducked his head, disappearing down the companionway. She didn't realize she was holding her breath until he reappeared and looked at her.

"Prove it."

She opened her mouth but didn't know what to say.

"Erik and Rory's wedding is on Saturday," he added. "I'm standing up for him. I'll pick you up at three."

"Crashing a wedding is even worse than crashing an anniversary party!"

His lips twisted. "Suit yourself." He ducked his head again.

"Wait!"

He straightened again, his gaze steady. She moistened her lips and the toe of her shoe bumped up against the edge of the ramp stretching over the water to his boat. "What would I need to wear?" It was the very last thing she cared about, yet it was the only thing that came to her lips.

"I think *clothing* is the accepted norm," he deadpanned.

She made a face. "Is it formal? Semiformal? Casual? You just said you're his best man. Are you wearing a suit or a tux?"

"Suit. And if you need more details than that, I'll give you Rory's phone number and you can ask her. I suppose you went to work yesterday instead of taking the day off like the doc suggested."

The comment came out of nowhere and her shoulders tightened. "I had a story to turn in." And fat lot of good that had done. She might as well have stayed home and saved herself from the up-close dose of Harvey's wrath.

"You call and make that appointment with her?"

"No. But I will," she added quickly. "Tomorrow." She moistened her lips again. "First thing."

He watched her as if he were trying to decide whether or not to trust what she'd said. Then he nodded abruptly. "Any time's okay except Wednesday mornings," he said before disappearing below deck once again.

She hesitated uncertainly. Was he going to reappear? Did he expect her to leave? *Want* her to leave?

She knew she probably should, but reluctance to do so had her ignoring common sense and stepping onto the ramp instead. She wrapped her fingers around the rope that was stretched along its length for a handhold and tried not to wonder how deep the water was below.

She had only seen *Honey Girl* from a distance until now. Her gaze ranged over the wealth of gleaming, polished wood, and she knew that if she ran her hand along the rail, the wood would be as satiny and warm as living flesh.

Don't you mean as warm as Pax's flesh?

Her grip tightened on the rope. "I'll call and let you know when the appointment is," she said loudly.

The only answer she got was a thud from below deck and what sounded like an oath.

Concerned, she hustled across the ramp and stepped carefully into the boat. She was probably breaking nautical protocol by going aboard without permission, but she didn't care and quickly headed down the narrow steps into the cabin.

But all Pax was doing was standing there studying a large pad. Then his hooded gaze slid over her. "What's wrong?"

Besides everything? "Nothing. I thought I heard a noise."

He didn't answer as he tore off the top sheet from the pad and rolled it into a tube that he secured with a rubber band he pulled from one of the built-in cupboards that surrounded the cozy space.

She shifted, feeling awkward. "Anyway, I'll let you know about the appointment."

He tossed the tube on the upholstered bunk, which was covered in fabric that reminded her painfully of the cushions they'd slept on together. "You said."

He *had* heard her then. She felt even more foolish and then compounded it by jumping a little when he suddenly stepped close.

Her nerves prickled as she looked up at him, and they went into overdrive completely when his hand closed over her shoulder. Heat spread through her veins like wildfire.

But all he did was nudge her to one side. "You're blocking." He lifted the pad.

Her cheeks went hot, and she sidled out of the way so he could slide the drawing pad into a narrow cupboard clearly designed to hold such things. She'd heard that pregnancy hormones increased a woman's libido, but this was ridiculous. She rubbed her moist palms on the back of her jeans. "You don't usually dock *Honey Girl* here, do you?"

"Port Orchard. My folks still have a place on the water there. I brought *Honey Girl* over so Patrice could get a feel for her." He waited a beat as if he expected some reaction from her. "She wants something similar," he finished.

The light outside was dwindling and it had started to sprinkle. She'd never really needed a cold shower before, but it was appealing now. If only it would just pour instead of drizzle. "Patrice is the—" She gestured vaguely to the open air behind him.

"Prospective client," he provided blandly.

Either the redhead had a heck of a job, or she was independently wealthy. A Merrick & Sullivan yacht did not come inexpensively. But it did explain the drawing pad because Shea knew that he often sat with a new client and sketched ideas before a design was selected. "How long will it take to finish the commission?"

"Have to finalize a sale before we can worry about that." He lowered his arms and straightened, suddenly seeming to take up even more space. And he was completely blocking the path to freedom.

She moistened her lips. "Cornelia doesn't know I'm pregnant, does she? Why didn't you say that you hadn't told her?"

"You'd already decided that I had. Would you have believed me?"

He had a point. "She wants me to do more work for her." She wasn't sure what prompted her to share that, but as soon as she did, she knew she wanted his opinion.

"More vetting?"

"As one of the associates there." She hesitated. "You know. Reading the letters and helping choose…projects."

"Shea, the fairy godmother," he murmured.

"It's ridiculous. I know." She pushed her tangled hair back from her face and pulled in a quick breath. "I'm sorry I upset you the other night."

His expression didn't change. "Upset is one word for it." He flicked open his coat and lifted his arm, hooking his fingers over one of the latches on an upper cabinet near his head. "But you haven't changed your mind about anything."

The gray T-shirt he wore beneath the jacket was stretched to the limit across his hard chest. She dragged her eyes away. "I know some things will change."

His lips twisted.

"Obviously, I don't have the proper room for a baby in my apartment right now," she added.

"I don't care if you ever have room," he said. "I want you living somewhere safer."

"I can't afford to move!"

"Moving in with me doesn't cost you a dime. In fact, it will save you rent altogether."

Alarm bells started clanging inside her head. "Move *in* with you," she repeated stupidly. As *what?* His lover? His roommate?

"And I can damn sure promise that the cops don't have reason to come calling at my place three times a day," he added.

"I can't move in with you!"

His brief smile was sardonic. "Can't isn't the same thing as won't."

"I don't need an English lesson!"

"You told Bea I had an equal say where our son was concerned. So you're saying you didn't mean that after all?"

She let out a consternated huff. "Yes, I meant it."

His expression hardened. "Then you said it, figuring you'd never have to worry about it because you're certain I'm gonna book sooner or later."

Wasn't that exactly what she was afraid of? "No," she denied, sounding strangled. She cleared the knot from her throat. "I said it because I meant it."

"Then *I* say, I want you under my roof."

Her legs felt unsteady. She wanted to blame it on the rhythmic rocking of the water beneath the boat, but the faint motion was much more soothing than agitating. "Do you really think that's wise?"

He lifted an eyebrow, waiting.

"Things are complicated enough without us—" She pulled in another steadying breath. "Endingupinbedtogether," she said on a rush.

His head dipped toward her and his voice dropped. "Afraid you won't be able to control yourself?"

She felt surrounded by him. By his height. By his scent. By *him*. And it infuriated her—because he knew it.

She could see it in his eyes. In the devilish quirk at the corner of his infernally perfect mouth.

Her common sense snapped right in two.

She angled her chin, shaking her hair back as she slid her hand behind his head and pulled it down.

"Can *you*?" she whispered and pressed her mouth to his.

Chapter Nine

The best-laid plans.

The thought was fleeting in Pax's head, rapidly shoved aside by the taste of Shea.

Her lips, seductive and greedily sweet, moved across his, and he had as little defense against them now as when she'd kissed him during the ice storm.

He pushed his fingers through her hair, tilting her head further so he could deepen the kiss, and she made a low, approving sound that went straight down his spine. Her lips parted and her tongue danced, and his self-control snapped.

He ran his mouth down the side of her neck and felt her hands yank at his shirt, thrusting beneath to press against his skin. She groaned and twisted her head until she found his mouth again, and he yanked off her jacket, filling his hands with her breasts.

She let out a soft cry and her head fell back. He could

feel her shaking, and he mindlessly backed up until he felt the bunk behind him. He fell onto it, pulling her down over him and dragging her shirt upward, letting his eyes feast before he pulled aside the sheer fabric of her bra, baring her creamy skin to his mouth.

She jerked, breathing his name.

Her hair tumbled around him as she straightened her arms against the bunk and arched against his mouth. She was coming undone right beneath his hands, and he clamped his fingers around her rocking hips, urging her on.

She suddenly cried out, shuddering wildly, and he groaned, scrambling for some control, but it was already beyond him. He reached between them and worked down her zipper, delving beneath her silky panties, and she bowed her head over his, arching into his hand.

But the moment his fingertips found her sweet heat, she froze.

Jerked back.

She suddenly planted her hand on his chest and pushed up, nearly unmanning him with her knee as she untangled her legs from his and scrambled to her feet, yanking up her zipper.

Her eyes were round and wide, her lips rosy and her breasts tauntingly displayed.

As if realizing it, she tugged her bra into place and pulled her beige shirt down to her hips. "I can't believe I let this happen again!"

He was hard and ached to his back teeth for her. But the horror in her eyes kept his hands to himself.

"You kissed me, sweetheart," he reminded. He levered off the bunk, and even though he'd built the boat himself, had taken her out too many times to count, he still managed to slam his head into the overhead locker. He muttered an oath and headed for the steps.

The sooner he got out on deck in the open air, the better his chances were of not losing his mind entirely.

She was hard on his heels, fumbling into her jacket. "Yes, because I was trying to prove a point!"

"Not get naked and have hot crazy sex on my boat?" He slammed the hatch closed and grabbed a perfectly coiled rope, coiling it all over again just to keep from reaching for her—whether to convince her to finish what they'd started, or to throttle her, he wasn't sure. "Maybe if we stopped trying to prove our points, we could start working together!" He flung aside the rope and it slithered right over the side and into the water.

She caught the end before the whole length could go overboard and silently held it out. Her hand was shaking.

He took it, avoiding even the slightest graze against her hand, and jerked the rest of the rope out of the water, hunting for the patience that he usually had in abundance. She'd thrown him one hell of a curveball. But he was damned if he'd lose sight of the entire ballgame.

Namely her, and their baby, in his life.

Period.

"I don't want to have to worry about you living alone over at that place," he said flatly. "If you get *sick,*" he added pointedly. "If something goes wrong. If somebody breaks in while you're sleeping. I don't—" He stopped and took a deep breath. Let it out and flipped the rope into another practiced coil. "I don't give a damn what kind of money you have or don't have, what you can or cannot afford or whether it is *wise.*" Finished with the rope, he jammed it over its hook. "I want you to be where I can take care of you. You're having my kid for Christ's sake!" He finally looked at her. "Is it that unnatural that his parents happen to have the hots for each other?"

The rain was more mist than drops, and in the dwindling sunlight it settled in sparkles all over her hair as the silence between them lengthened.

Then she suddenly lifted her hand and jabbed her finger toward him, though it was none too steady. "I'm not going to do your laundry," she said abruptly.

He went still. "What?"

Her eyes avoided his. "A-and if I cook, you're cleaning up afterward," she added.

Maybe he'd conked his head harder than he'd thought, or all of his blood was still occupied elsewhere, because he'd gone strangely lightheaded. "You'll move into my apartment."

Her jaw slanted. She dropped her hand. "How could I refuse when you ask so nicely?"

"Pardon me if I sound a little too cranky for your liking."

She flushed brightly. "I'm sorry. I never intended—"

He cut her off, not exactly in the mood to hear her stumbling excuse. "When?" he demanded.

She threw her hands in the air. "I don't know! I have to give notice at my apartment and pack, and—" She broke off and brushed her hand over her forehead. "Marsha-Marsha is not going to be happy about this." Her gaze flew back to his. "And you have a dog." She said it like it was the worst possible sin.

But there was no way he was going to let her slip away now. "Hooch is a friendly dog." That was true. "Gets along great with cats." That was possibly true. He didn't know because Hooch had never spent any time with cats before.

"Really?" Her tone dripped with sudden suspicion. "They'll be cooped up all day in the same space."

"Not all day. I take Hooch out mornings and nights." And he had a dog walker who came during the afternoon.

"But it's still an apartment."

"Then I'll buy a freakin' house," he countered flatly. "With a big-ass yard." He wasn't going to admit to her he'd already been looking any more than he wanted to admit to himself that he kept picturing her living there with him. "Plenty of space for Hooch and the baby to play."

Panic slid over her face.

He'd gone too far and he wanted to swear a blue streak.

"Or we'll stay in Belltown," he revised abruptly. "There's an extra bedroom at my place. Marsha-Marsha can have it all to herself. Hooch'll never bother her."

She chewed the inside of her lip. "And if I want the extra bedroom?"

He exhaled, blowing out his frustration, because there was no denying the uncertainty written on her face. "Do you?" It was no secret which arrangement *he* preferred, and he'd be damned if he'd pretend otherwise.

"I don't know," she whispered.

It was an honest answer, at least, even if it wasn't the one his aching gut wanted. "Let's just get your stuff moved," he said gruffly. "And take it from there."

She gnawed on her lip for a moment. "Okay. But I don't still need to go with you to your partner's wedding, right?"

He smiled. He'd probably regret the genuine pleasure he took in her discomfort. "What do you think?"

"Are you a friend of the bride?"

Shea looked away from the two men standing at the front of the small Port Orchard chapel to the carrot-topped woman who'd slid into the pew next to her.

"Sort of," she whispered back. Shea had only met Rory the night before at the small rehearsal dinner held in Seattle. She didn't think that one dinner with Rory and a half dozen other people would qualify her as a friend, but neither did interviewing the groom a handful of times.

The wedding hadn't yet officially begun, and Erik and
Pax were talking to the people taking up the first several
pews. Naturally some of them were Erik's family members, but Shea was surprised at how many of them were
related to Pax. She looked at the woman beside her again.
"You?"

"I'll be selling my handmade candles when Rory opens
the Harbor Market for the season."

The market, Shea had also learned the night before,
was the seasonal business that Cornelia had helped Rory
take over shortly before she'd hired Shea. The place had
belonged to Erik's grandparents and he'd handled the sale
for them as well as worked with Rory to get the business
reestablished and ready for operation come spring.

She also now realized that Erik and Rory were one of
Cornelia's "happy coincidences." Shea figured the only
reason Cornelia wasn't there to beam her personal ap-
proval was because Harry had whisked her to New York
for the weekend. Cornelia hadn't even been in her office
for Shea's usual Friday check-in.

It was just as well.

When Shea hadn't been working on one of Harvey's assignments, she'd been busy sorting and packing all of her
belongings to move in with Pax. Not much time had been
left to read the material Cornelia had given her. And if the
few requests that she had managed to read so far were any
indication, she wasn't holding out much hope she'd find
any pieces of gold among the dross.

Pax and Erik took their positions as the strains of a vio-
lin began and the low murmur of people talking died away.

Since Gloria had divorced Shea's father, she'd been at
every one of her mother's subsequent weddings. She knew
her attention was supposed to be on the bride and the
groom, and she tried. She really did.

Erik's eyes were glued to his intended, who seemed to float along the chapel's short aisle, holding the hand of her little boy, Tyler. He was trying to maintain a solemn expression, though his face kept splitting into a wide grin that showed off a missing front tooth.

But Shea's focus kept turning to Pax, who looked taller than ever and unfairly handsome in a dark, pinstriped suit. He was also plainly pleased for his friend and partner and clearly relaxed.

Which was more than she could say for herself.

She felt like she was wound tighter than a cheap watch.

She'd thrown herself at him. And even though he hadn't mentioned that fact the few times they'd spoken on the phone since then, or when he'd picked her up for the rehearsal dinner the night before, *she* couldn't put it out of her mind.

He wasn't even going along with any sort of normal time frame to move from her home into his. He'd arranged for the movers to come the next morning. And she, try as she might, couldn't come up with a valid reason to stop them.

By this time tomorrow, Shea Weatherby would be living under Paxton Merrick's roof.

He'd told his family.

Everyone had seemed delighted. Including Beatrice. She was sitting next to Shea now, and Pax's parents were in the pew in front of them. The chapel was just this side of minuscule. Shea figured there were about forty people present, with at least ten standing in the back. She'd have been happy to be one of them, where escape was within easy reach.

Rory and Erik had turned to face one another to share their vows. Even though Shea had been through these events a half dozen times, the emotion in their voices made her throat tighten. There was no question they were deeply in love. She only hoped for their sake that it would last.

Her gaze snuck back to Pax, only to find him watching her.

She wanted to run and hide. Something she couldn't possibly do. Not with Candle Lady on one side of her and Pax's sister on the other. She finally got a reprieve when he had to turn his own attention back to his best man duties and produce the wedding ring he'd been keeping in his pocket.

Linda suddenly turned to look at her over the back of the pew. Her eyes were misty. "Maybe the next wedding in this chapel will be yours and Pax's," she whispered.

Shea smiled weakly.

And then everyone was standing, clapping and laughing because the minister had just presented the new mister and missus, and young Tyler had given a fist-pumping *"yes."*

Gloria had always loved leaving the church on the arm of her latest, shiny new husband without really stopping to chat with the guests. Probably because the grand exit assured her of being the absolute center of attention.

But Rory and Erik weren't doing anything of the sort. They were stopping and talking and laughing with everyone along the way until it seemed as if all the guests were part of the exodus out the double doors. And the rain gods were smiling upon them—the sky was a perfect robin's egg blue without a cloud in sight.

Shea knew that Pax was working his way toward her, but she still trembled when he slid his hand around her waist before nudging her forward into the departing throng. He bent down until his mouth was near her ear. "Imagine that. You survived crashing a wedding without the walls falling in."

She dared a quick glance at him. "You may want to be a stand-up comedian, but don't quit your day job."

His dimple flashed.

Her stomach swooped.

And she knew she was in for a long night.

If Shea hadn't already realized how close Erik's and Pax's families were, she got a clue when they migrated to the reception, which was being held under a tent on the lawn behind Linda and Daniel's house. They'd insisted on it, since Erik's parents had moved to California some time ago. They were even going to watch Tyler for the next week so the newlyweds could get away for a honeymoon.

Given the clear skies and beautiful sunset, nobody stayed under the tent for long. Particularly after the toasts had been made, the sumptuous meal had been served and the dancing started.

Now, Shea was sitting off to the side at one of the round tables that had been dragged out from under the tent, and everywhere she looked there were smiles and laughter and hugs and children running around with wedding cake smeared on their faces.

Beneath the table, she slipped her feet out of the high-heeled pumps she'd bought the day before during a mad dash through the mall. They pinched her toes but on the mannequin they'd looked like the perfect match for the pale blue floaty dress Shea had ended up buying. She hadn't wanted to brave another trip to her mother's closet. She hardly shared all the details of her life with Gloria, but she'd been afraid that, face to face, she wouldn't be able to refrain from telling her she was moving in with Pax.

And why.

She had enough doubts without adding a heaping helping of her mother on top of them.

"Here." Beatrice returned from the buffet table with

two drinks in her hand, setting one next to Shea's elbow. "Orange juice," she said. "Purely virginal."

"Thanks." Shea took a sip, nodding toward Rory and Erik, who were swaying together several yards away. "They make a pretty couple," she murmured. Pax was dancing too, with his mother. But the sight of them was almost too much to take. She couldn't forget just how well he could move. And wouldn't it figure that he'd also know how to waltz?

"They do." Beatrice propped her elbow on the table and cupped her chin on her hand. "When I was thirteen, I had a terrible crush on Erik." Her lips tilted. "I even cornered him in the boathouse once and kissed him." She pointed to the building that jutted out over the water and chuckled. "He was eighteen and said if I ever pulled a stupid stunt like that again, he'd toss me off the dock. Fortunately, I realized during the whole debacle that kissing him was about as appealing as kissing my brother. Definitely not a great love affair in the making." She laughed and lowered her voice. "I didn't have a *clue* how great kissing could be until I went off to college and met my roommate's brother, Trey." She sat back and fanned herself with her hand. "Haven't met a man yet who could live up to the way that man kissed."

Shea sipped her juice, looking over the glass at Pax. She hadn't known what kissing was about either until she'd met him. And she was quite certain he couldn't be surpassed. But she didn't necessarily want to share that particular fact with the man's sister.

When he suddenly approached, she nearly choked and quickly set the glass back on the table.

"Come on," he said, extending his hand. "You're not getting off scot-free here."

"I don't really dance," she excused quickly.

"Oh, go on." Beatrice nudged her. "It's a wedding. Everyone has to dance." To prove it, she hopped off her chair and nabbed Erik's gray-haired grandfather as he passed by and pulled him toward the dancers.

Shea looked up at Pax, unaccountably nervous at the notion of dancing with him. Which was silly, considering. "My shoes pinch." She gathered her sweater around her as she leaned sideways and waved a bare foot where he could see.

His half smile was knowing and he didn't lower his hand. "So don't wear them." With his deep, assured voice, he was the soul of reason. "You are going to dance with me, so just deal with it. And try not to grumble too much," he added. "It's a wedding. Everyone should be smiling."

She shot him a look and stuffed her feet back into her shoes.

"Thought they pinched," he murmured against her ear when she rose and took his hand.

She ignored him as he led her around to the far edge of the crowd before turning her into his arms. She knew immediately there was going to be no sedate waltzing with a respectable amount of space between their bodies.

No. This was full on, body-to-body contact, only vertical and clothed.

"Relax," he murmured, rubbing his hand down her spine. "You're thinking again."

"Not thinking enough is what got us here, remember?" But her hands were already sliding around his neck of their own accord, and her head had found a spot against his chest that seemed made for it.

Off to the side, she could see Pax's parents' house, brightly lit and welcoming, situated at the top of the gently sloped lawn where they were dancing. He'd grown up in that house. Had never lived anywhere else until he'd left home for school.

She couldn't imagine how that felt. Every one of her mother's marriages had included a new house. A new neighborhood. And after each divorce, it had been the same. A new apartment. A new school.

She pushed the thoughts away, trying to concentrate on something else, but the feel of his body against her made thinking about anything at all a challenge.

"The toast you gave for Erik and Rory was nice," she finally blurted. Actually, it *had* been lovely, and she hadn't been the only one who'd been moved by it. "Didn't you ever worry about ruining your friendship by going into business together?"

"Nope."

She angled her head back so she could see his face. A faint breeze was drifting over them and she heard the far-off moan of a ship's horn. "*Never?*"

His eyes were steady. "Isn't there anything in your life that you knew, absolutely knew, was the right thing for you? That you didn't doubt? Didn't second guess?"

She'd never doubted that he was more than she could handle.

"Journalism," she answered quickly. "I knew I wanted to be a journalist. Not that what I do for the *Tub* would qualify," she added darkly. "If Harvey knew I was going to be here, he'd have passed out from excitement thinking he'd be in for an exclusive on Erik's wedding."

Pax tilted his head, giving the wrapped bodice of her dress an openly considering look. "You have a digital camera tucked down your dress like you did that pen?"

Despite everything, a laugh bubbled up. "Harvey's not getting anything from me. Not this time."

"Damn." His dimple appeared. "I don't have an excuse to go camera diving."

Shivers rippled down her spine. "Nope." She was vaguely

aware of the music sliding from one dreamy song into another and highly aware of the press of his fingertips dipping toward the small of her back.

She clung a little desperately to the most unromantic thing she could think of.

"Harvey was the only one who hired me." Despite her better intention, her head found that spot on Pax's chest again and she ached inside when his arms seemed to tighten around her. "And I applied *everywhere*."

"You've got more experience to put on your resume now. If you really want to leave, do it."

She made a soft sound. "Probably not the best time for job hopping."

"Being pregnant, you mean." His soft words brushed against her temple and his thighs moved slowly against hers.

She exhaled shakily. Sensation trounced common sense. "Mmm-hmm."

"You wouldn't have to work at all if you didn't want to."

She shook her head, though rubbing her cheek against the warmth radiating from him was probably the real motive. She forced herself to stop. To lift her head so there was at least one part of her not plastered against him.

She realized he'd danced her farther away from the others than she realized. "I'm not going to be your kept woman, Pax, if that's what you're getting at."

His head lowered and she felt his lips against her cheek. "'Baby mama' doesn't fly for you?"

She slowly shook her head.

"What about 'wife'?"

Something inside her chest fisted.

Beatrice had warned her he'd head in that direction.

She pulled back again as far as his arm surrounding

her would allow, which wasn't far. "Getting married just because I'm pregnant is a bad idea. We already agreed."

"I didn't agree," he said quietly. "I just didn't choose to debate the issue with you."

She didn't know why she was tearful all of a sudden. But she was, and there was no way he could fail to notice. "Please don't do this here," she whispered thickly.

He lifted one hand, touching her cheek gently. "Shea."

Tenderness from him would be her undoing. "You're supposed to be celebrating your best friend's wedding."

"I'm celebrating my best friend's *marriage*. Anyone can have a wedding. Erik and Rory are going to have something a lot more important. Something that lasts a lifetime."

"And maybe they'll get there," she conceded huskily. "Right now they love each other, at least. They're starting out with a better reason than pregnancy."

His feet stopped moving altogether, though he still held her close. "Why is it so hard for you to see what's right in front of your face?"

Her throat felt like a vise was tightening around it. "I don't want us to end up hating each other."

Despite the dim lighting, his eyes searched hers, leaving her feeling raw. Exposed.

"There's no rule that says we will."

"And I don't want—" she broke off, striving for composure "—this baby having the kind of childhood I had."

"You're already lining up a half dozen prospective husbands?" His tone was gently teasing. He brushed away a tear she hadn't even realized was sliding down her cheek. "Ah, hell. You kill me when you do that," he murmured and brushed his mouth softly over hers. Then he kissed her cheek, cradled the back of her head in his hand and kissed her forehead before tugging her close again. "I don't want you to cry."

If he thought that was going to stop her, he was hugely mistaken. As she sniffled she was glad they were far enough away from the other guests that nobody was likely to notice. "My parents got married because of me." Her voice was muffled against his chest. "That's the only reason. It didn't last even a couple years and the only way I knew my father at all was because of the occasional visit he made, despite the hatred between them." Her fingers dug into his shoulders. "At least this way you and I can be...friends...and have some hope of staying that way." She looked up at him. "This baby can still grow up with both of us around."

He didn't answer right away. Just looked skyward for a moment and let out a long breath. "I guess that's a no on the proposal." His low voice was wry and her corkscrewed nerves unwound a notch. His arms tightened around her for a moment, and then he set her away, looking beyond her toward the others. "Looks like the happy couple's getting ready to leave. I'd better—"

"Of course." She pulled her sweater more tightly around herself, managing a quick smile. "Go on and say your goodbyes or whatever. I'll be along." He didn't look convinced and she gestured vaguely. "I'm just going to freshen up first." To prove it, she took a few steps in the direction of the house.

When she looked back, he was already striding toward Erik and Rory, scooping up a beer from somewhere and holding it aloft.

She swiped her hands over her damp cheeks.

She believed in her heart that she was right.

So why was it all suddenly feeling so very wrong?

Chapter Ten

"No, no, that box is going to the donation center." Shea hastily stepped out of the way of the hulking young guy carrying one of the last of her packing boxes toward the moving truck. "Could you put it in the trunk there?" She pointed to her car.

Somehow she'd managed to score a parking spot almost directly in front of her building, so she could more easily load up the stuff she intended to drop off at the thrift shop before driving to Pax's apartment in Belltown.

The mover dumped the box in her trunk and went back into the building. He had two others working with them, and it was daunting how quickly they'd emptied her apartment. The only things left up there were a half dozen boxes and Marsha-Marsha, whom she'd left unhappily contained in her crate tended by Gonzo next door.

She had a key to Pax's apartment tucked in her front pocket. He'd arrived at the same time the movers had, but he hadn't stayed for long. He'd just given her the key and security code, made sure the movers were doing what they were supposed to do and left again because he had a client meeting that had been moved up.

At least that's what he'd said.

She wasn't sure if it were an excuse or not and supposed—in the end—that it didn't matter. She didn't need him to be there holding her hand, after all. It was just a simple matter of overseeing the movers.

She sighed faintly as she went back inside the building and jabbed the button for the elevator. It figured that just when she was leaving, the darned thing would finally be running.

The door opened, emitting another one of her movers; this one pushing a handcart with several boxes stacked on it. He nodded at her as they traded places. "Nearly done, ma'am. My guys have t' have a lunch break and then we'll be ready to deliver."

The word struck her and she barely kept her hand from pressing flat against her abdomen. "That's fine. I'll be there all afternoon." The elevator doors closed between them, and a few creaking seconds later they let her out again on her floor.

Gonzo was sitting in the hallway, his back against the wall between their apartment doors. Marsha-Marsha's crate sat between his bent knees and he'd stuck a finger through the plastic slats to pet her. "You know anything about boat guy's sailing camp?"

Pax had a sailing camp? She shook her head. "No. Why?"

He lifted a brochure that she hadn't noticed sitting beside him on the floor and held it out. "He left this with my mom when he was here this morning."

Pax had come and gone in a matter of minutes. He'd

even spoken more with the movers than he had with her. If those few words he had allotted her hadn't clearly displayed his satisfaction over her moving, she would have feared he'd begun having the same doubts as she.

She took the glossy pamphlet from Gonzo and unfolded it, quickly reading about the sailing camp aimed at under-privileged youth. Which Gonzo definitely was. His single mother worked days in a dry cleaner's and took college classes online at night.

She looked at him. "Are you interested in learning how to sail?"

"I dunno. Maybe." The boy lifted his shoulder. "My ma says I have to do something after school's out."

"Well." She handed him back the brochure. "I'm sure you'd enjoy it. I had a stepdad who took me sailing once. Once I got over being afraid because I didn't know how to swim, it was a lot of fun."

"Boat guy doesn't take you on his boat?"

She shook her head, not wanting to think too hard about what had occurred between them on *Honey Girl.* "It says on the brochure that the enrollment is limited. If you're really thinking about it, you should sign up soon."

Two movers came out of her apartment, each wielding a big box.

"I suppose that's the last of it?"

The older of the two nodded. "You want to check around and make sure. Then Joey'll have a paper for you to sign." He didn't wait around for her response but headed for the elevator, probably already thinking about his lunch break.

She pulled out the ten dollars she'd promised Gonzo for watching Marsha-Marsha for her while the movers were there and handed it to him, then leaned over and wrapped her hand around the handle of Marsha-Marsha's crate. She could feel the cat scrambling around in the small confines when she picked it up. "You take care of yourself and your mom, okay, Gonzo?"

He pushed to his feet and nodded. He was clutching the sailing camp brochure in one hand and the ten in his other. "See ya." He disappeared into his apartment.

She blew out a breath. She was surprised to realize how much she was going to miss him. Earsplitting music and all.

She went back into her apartment. It was so small that she really could see if she'd forgotten anything in one single glance. But she walked around the perimeter anyway. "Remember when we first came here, Marsha?" She lifted the crate and looked in on her cat. "I think it took you a week before you came out from under the couch."

The cat eyed her and meowed plaintively.

"Sounds like she does not like her crate."

Shea whirled to see Beatrice standing in the open doorway and took an instinctive step toward her. "What's wrong? Is Pax okay?"

Beatrice's eyebrows shot up. She waved her hands as she came through the door. "Relax. Nothing's wrong. Pax is fine. He asked me to come over and be with you since he couldn't." She pushed up the sleeves of her skinny black turtleneck and smiled. "But I can see I'm a little late."

"Why would he do that?"

"Duh. Because he didn't want you to be alone." Beatrice's eyes were full of good humor.

Shea blinked rapidly, but it didn't help. She still felt weepy. "I don't know what's wrong with me," she told Beatrice, trying for wry and missing by a mile. "Every time I turn around, I'm—"

"Pregnant," Beatrice inserted. She dropped her purse on the breakfast bar and wrapped her arms around Shea's shoulders, giving her a hug. "Hormones, sweetie. I hear they can be a bitch."

"I don't even know why I'm going to miss this place. The walls are too thin, and the plumbing—" She laughed brokenly. "Well, it hardly bears thinking about. It *was* a crapshack, but it was my crapshack."

Beatrice gave her another squeeze, then pulled back. "Frankly, I'd be crying if I were moving in with Pax." She gave a mock shudder. "Happier living with Grammy and Granddad. Let me carry that for you." She took the crate without waiting and lifted it until she could see inside. "Hooch is going to *love* you, kitty."

Shea went into the kitchen and tore off a paper towel from the roll she'd left there and wiped her face.

"Mom is going to meet us at Pax's with lunch," Beatrice said. She looked over at Shea. "Hope that's all right with you. She's dumping off cake from the reception last night on any and all takers."

What could Shea possibly say? "That cake was pretty delicious."

Beatrice's eyes twinkled. If she knew how uneasy Shea felt, she hid it well. "I figure it's worth an extra spin class or two." She stepped out into the hall and waited while Shea locked the door behind them, then they walked down the hall to the elevator.

Inside, Shea punched the button for the ground floor. "I could probably count on one hand the number of times this elevator has worked since I moved in."

"Pax mentioned he talked to the building super about it."

The elevator pinged, but Shea barely heard. She stared at Beatrice. "Pax had something to do with this thing getting fixed?"

Beatrice made a face and adjusted her grip on the cat

carrier. "I'm guessing I've said something he didn't want me saying." The elevator doors slid open and she stepped out. "You didn't know."

"No," she said faintly.

Joey, the head mover, was waiting there for her and shoved a clipboard and pen in front of her as soon as she stepped off the elevator after Beatrice. She scratched her signature at the bottom of the smudged paper and handed him back his pen. "Thanks."

"Sure thing, ma'am." His appreciative gaze lingered on Beatrice as he headed outside where his associates were already waiting in the truck.

"You have an admirer," she told Beatrice and then held up her key. "I need to turn this in. I can meet you at Pax's if you want to go on ahead."

"I took the metro over. He warned me parking was terrible here. Go ahead. I'll wait, then we can ride together, if you don't mind giving me a ride."

Shea walked around to the manager's unit and left her key in the drop box. She would have liked a chance to question him more about the elevator business, but he wasn't in. When she rejoined Beatrice, Marsha-Marsha was even more restless. "I can take her."

"We're fine," Beatrice assured her and headed out the door. "Did I tell you that I landed two more jobs as a result of the Fresh Grounds event?" she asked once they were situated inside Shea's car.

"No." As she drove away, Shea watched the building for a moment in her rearview mirror. Was she really going to miss the place or just the independence that it represented?

She stopped at a red light and glanced at Beatrice. "More fundraisers?"

"One is. The other's a huge wedding."

"I'm sorry we didn't get the story run on the auction."

Beatrice lifted her shoulder and smiled slightly. "Not the end of the world. The auction made twenty percent more than they'd hoped, and that was the point of the event in the first place. All in all, I am perfectly pleased with the results."

"Even without media coverage." No other outlets had mentioned the auction either.

Beatrice gave her a calm smile that was uncannily like her brother's. "Even without," the other woman assured blithely. Then she nodded toward the windshield. "Light's green."

Fresh butterflies danced inside Shea's stomach. She still wasn't sure what madness had made her agree to move in with Pax. But now that she had, there'd been no turning back.

So she ignored the fluttery little buggers and drove through the intersection.

The second Pax opened the door to his apartment that evening, he knew Shea was there. Not just because Beatrice had called to let him know when she and their mother had left Shea, or because of the way his nerves twitched, but because Hooch wasn't standing in the foyer, wagging his tail so hard his whole body shook.

Pax closed the door and set his keys on the narrow table in the hallway. He saw three packing boxes stacked against the wall, still taped closed. He walked past them and headed quietly into the living area. No boxes there. Nothing new at all.

Except Shea and her cat.

One was perched on top of the bookcase, warily watching him as he entered. The other was curled up in the corner of his couch, sound asleep with her hair streaming like a waterfall over the couch's arm. Hooch was stretched out beside Shea, taking up most of the real estate, which undoubtedly explained the cat's climb to safer territory. Though he looked at Pax, the dog clearly wasn't interested enough in his human's arrival to bother moving his head away from its resting place on Shea's thigh.

Pax rounded the couch and reached down to scratch the dog's head. "So much for devotion, eh?"

Hooch's tail flopped a few times.

"I don't blame you, buddy, believe me."

Shea had found the throw that Pax's housekeeper, Graciela, usually kept folded and stored away inside a cupboard. He pulled the edge of it up over her slender shoulder, resisting the urge to touch her in any other way. The television was turned to an old black-and-white movie with the volume low, and he left it undisturbed and went into the kitchen.

Either his mother had come bearing a helluva lot more than lunch, or Shea had made dinner. A big bowl of plastic-wrapped spaghetti was sitting on the counter, and when he touched the side of it, it was still warm. He pulled open the package wrapped in foil that sat beside it, letting out the mouthwatering scent of bread and garlic. He tugged off a piece and shoved it in his mouth.

"I didn't hear you come in."

He looked over and saw Shea with the blue throw draped around her shoulders. The only light in the kitchen came from the small bulb turned on over the stove. In the dimness, she looked sleepy-eyed and soft, and he felt such a stab of longing that he almost choked on the bread.

He snatched open the fridge and grabbed a bottle of beer he didn't really want, except as an excuse to keep his hands safely occupied. "You were sleeping. I see the cat's found a safe spot on top of the bookcase." He pushed the refrigerator door closed and twisted open the bottle top.

She made a soft sound. "Sorry about that. She made a beeline there the second I took her out of her crate. So far, she's totally ignoring her own cat tree. I put it in the extra room."

He stifled a sigh. "You don't have to be sorry. She'll get used to Hooch in time."

"I suppose." She took a hesitant step into the kitchen. "The food your doing?"

"I had so much left over from your shopping spree last week. I just packed it all up and brought it here."

"You didn't leave the dishes." Her brows pulled together and he gestured toward the empty sink with the bottle. "You said if you cooked, I cleaned up," he reminded and tried not to think too much about what had preceded that particular conversation.

Her lashes lowered as she walked the rest of the way into the room. Her cheeks were red. "I figured I owed you one," she murmured. She reached out and fiddled with the plastic wrap covering the pasta. "You're the reason the elevator is working."

He didn't have to work hard to realize what she meant. "I see my sister still talks a lot."

She pressed her hands around the sides of the bowl, smoothing the plastic back in place. "It was very nice of you."

He waited a beat. "But unnecessary?"

"Only if you did it to benefit me. Since I'm…here. But the hundred or so other people still living there are pretty happy." She finally looked at him. "But you needn't have sent your sister to make sure I actually got here."

"I asked Bea to go over because I didn't like leaving you to deal with moving on your own." Forestalling any possible argument, he added, "Not because I didn't think you could. Or that I was worried you'd decide not to come."

Her jaw canted. "You really had a client meeting?"

"Three, actually. Sundays aren't usually so busy." He tugged his tie loose and pulled a fork from the drawer. Then he slid the bowl away from her lax fingers and sat down on one of the barstools before peeling back the plastic wrap and sticking his fork in.

She made a sound. "Ever heard of a plate?" She opened an overhead cupboard and pulled out one of his white plates. She set it pointedly in front of him. "Don't worry," she said dryly. "I'll wash it."

He grinned and dumped a healthy portion onto the plate.

"Does it need warming?"

He shook his head and dug his fork back into the noodles. "Too much time. I'm starving." Better to feed his growling stomach than the other hunger plaguing him.

She took the cheesy garlic bread and sliced off a hunk, nudging it onto the side of his plate. Then she filled a glass with water and sipped at it as she leaned back against the sink. The city lights glittered through the big window behind her.

He dragged his eyes away from her and focused on the food. "Bread's good. You get it at that little bakery on the corner?"

"I made it." Her gaze skittered over his and then away. "I saw the bread maker you had in the pantry when I was putting things away. I stuck my cookbooks in there, too. I...hope you don't mind."

"Didn't even know I had a bread maker." He picked up his beer again, his brain tripping along a path paved with homemade bread and other wonders. "Probably my mother's doing. Who knows what else is lurking in the cupboards that she's decided I have to have."

"Your *mother?*" Her voice dripped skepticism and his happy little trip screeched to a standstill.

He studied her for a moment. "Who else do you think would be equipping me with kitchen appliances? One of those legions of women you seem to think I've had?"

She lifted one hand peaceably. "I shouldn't have said anything."

"I have never once brought another woman here who hasn't been a relation," he said evenly. "Until you."

She made an impatient sound and set aside her water glass. "You don't have to spin fairy tales for me, Pax. It's none of my business who you've...entertained here. It doesn't matter—"

"The hell it doesn't." He set the bottle down again with a careful clink. "Why do you find it so flippin' difficult to believe anything I say?"

She pressed her fingertip to the bridge of her nose for a moment. "This is silly." She dropped her hand. "If I'm actually going to live here, we probably should agree to just be honest. I don't need anything sugarcoated—"

"You *are* living here," he corrected flatly. "There's no way I'll ever be able to deny that I've enjoyed the company of plenty of women over the years. But not once have I ever told you something that wasn't truthful. I told you I haven't brought another woman here and—"

"I saw you!" she burst out. She pulled the throw off her shoulders and draped it over the back of the barstool tucked under the end of the counter, visibly gathering herself. "I saw you," she repeated more calmly. "On your last birthday. You were at the club right across the street from this very building."

"Koala's." He remembered his birthday perfectly well, including the fact that he had not had a date with him. Something that had earned him plenty of ribbing from his sister and cousins who'd celebrated with him.

"We ran the photo in the *Tub*," Shea added.

"I've been accused of possessing a healthy ego," he drawled, "but I don't recall my birthday being such hot news that it'd make a local paper."

Her lips tightened. "We were doing Harvey's annual list of favorite hotspots around the city. Koala's was number one."

"Yeah, they've been number one for years. So what?"

She looked even more annoyed. "So I was the one sitting outside nearly all night to get a photo of someone newsworthy coming in or out." She waved her hand. "And you and your three dates fit the bill to a tee," she finished flatly. "Unless you're going to claim they all coincidentally live in this building, too, I saw them come in with you."

"You and that pain-in-the-ass Harvey," he muttered and stomped out of the kitchen. He went into his study and grabbed a box off the top shelf and carried it back into the kitchen. He slapped the light switch, flooding the room with bright light.

Shea was still standing there looking uneasy. "Honestly, Pax. I told you it doesn't matter to me who you've had here in the past."

"Big of you." He dumped the box on the counter next to his plate and flipped off the lid. He rummaged through the newspaper clippings jumbled inside, found the one he wanted and slapped it on the counter between them. "That the one you're talking about?"

She warily stepped closer and glanced at it. "Yes." But she seemed more interested in the shoe box and slowly reached inside, pulling out another clipping. Then another. She held them in her hands. "These are all mine," she said slowly. "You've been saving—"

"No way, sweetheart. Don't change the subject." He planted his finger on the photograph she was damning him for and pushed it in front of her again. "Take another look, Shea."

"Oh, for Pete's—" She broke off and exhaled. "Fine." She looked at the clipping.

"Who do you see?"

"You, obviously," she said tightly. "And count 'em. One, two, three blondes."

"You never went in the club that night, did you?"

She gave him a look. "The owner doesn't like his patrons' privacy disturbed. I couldn't even get past the bouncer."

"So you just took your little pictures and assumed the worst." He snatched up the clipping. "Take another look at the faces, Shea, before you go accusing me of lying again."

Shea tugged the clipping he was waving in front of her face out of his fingers.

Maybe Pax didn't think it was a big deal that he kept a shoe box containing the pieces she'd done at the *Tub,* but she was certainly distracted by it. The box was nearly full.

But it was easier to look at the clipping than it was to look at the storm brewing on his face, so she did. She took in the small, grainy newsprint photo. His head was thrown back in laughter, while his long arms were looped over his companions' shoulders. Beneath the photo, Harvey's top-10 list was printed.

She started to set the clipping back on the counter, but something made her stop. She moved her thumb away from the face of one of his dates and felt her stomach drop away.

"Jennifer," she realized aloud. The mother of the little blonde girl with lopsided pigtails. And Pax's cousin.

The other two women, their faces less clear than Jennifer's, were familiar, too.

"Beatrice used to be blond?" She looked up at him. She didn't remember the third woman's name, but she was the one who'd claimed pickle juice was just the ticket for morning sickness.

Shea felt plenty sick, but she was certain no amount of juice was going to help right now.

Pax's eyes didn't waver from her face. "I don't lie," he said flatly.

She pressed her lips together. "I'm sorry. I just—"

"Thought the worst, as usual."

She dropped the clipping back into the box. It settled lightly on top of the others. "It was back in August. Long before we—" She swallowed hard and reached into the box, grabbed a handful of the newspaper clippings and dumped them on the counter. "How many other times are you seen with one woman or another?" She dashed her hand over the pieces, spreading them out. "Nine times out of ten you've had a date with you!" She held up an example before tossing it back into the box. "Don't blame me for not realizing the night of your birthday was any different!"

He exhaled. "I don't blame you for thinking it," he said tiredly. "I blame you for thinking I'm lying about it now."

"I'm sorry!"

"Yeah. You're sorry. And what happens the next time?" His eyes probed hers. "You *have* to start trusting me, Shea. I said you're the only woman I've ever brought here. You're the only one who has ever been pregnant with my child. You're the only one I—" He broke off and his teeth closed together like he was grinding them. "Forget it." He pushed away from the counter and headed out of the room.

She instinctively followed. "Pax, wait."

He was wearing a perfectly tailored gray suit. She could easily see the way his shoulders stiffened. But he stopped. Made a quarter turn and looked back at her.

"I'm sorry," she said again.

His lips twisted.

"Well, I am!" She rubbed her palms down the sides of her jeans. "This is new for me, all right? I've lived on my own since I was seventeen. I'm sorry if I'm doing everything wrong here!"

"It's new for me, too."

So she was realizing. She chewed the inside of her lip and watched him. "I don't know what to expect. What *you* expect."

"I expect you to start trusting me."

"I mean with this." She spread her hands, taking in the kitchen around them. "Living together. I know you said we'd figure things out along the way, but—" She broke off and tucked her hair behind her ears. Nobody but Pax had ever made her feel so nervous. "But there's no point in us pretending that you'd want me here if I weren't pregnant," she finished abruptly.

A muscle ticked in his jaw. "Really? I asked you to marry me the other night."

"That wasn't a proposal! It was a discussion. Again, only because of the baby."

Wasn't it?

She folded her arms tightly, as if she could strangle the question back out of her head.

"You've just admitted you don't bring women here," she continued doggedly. "The only thing different about me is that I'm pregnant. And…and you feel some sort of old-fashioned responsibility in taking care of me because of it."

"It's not old-fashioned in my book."

She moistened her lips. "Anyway, I just think everything would be easier if we, I don't know, if we didn't rely so much on figuring—" she unwound her arms to sketch quotation marks in the air "—things out along the way and agreed to some ground rules."

He raked his hands down his face. She wasn't sure if

he was wiping away frustration or anger. When he suddenly turned back into the kitchen and stepped toward her, she jumped.

But all he did was reach around her for his beer.

"Besides the embargo on our unmentionables comingling in the washing machine, you mean?" His gaze slid over her face. "You've already broken the whole cooking-slash-dishes thing. So far, you're not hitting it out of the park when it comes to your ability to follow your own rules."

She flushed.

He lifted the bottle and took a slow drink, but his eyes never veered from her face. "Fine. You want rules. Here are mine. Graciela comes in a couple times a week to clean and do the laundry and she'll do yours as well as mine." His gaze bored into hers. "Take the extra bedroom or not. Right now I actually don't care. You want to pretend this is just some roommate situation, go right ahead. But when you come to my bed, *and you will,* come knowing that's where you intend to stay."

Then he grabbed the plate of spaghetti, tucked the foil-wrapped loaf of bread under his arm and left the room.

Chapter Eleven

"Okay." Dr. Montgomery rolled back on her stool and smiled. "Everything is excellent. Just exactly the way it should look moving into your second trimester." She peeled off her gloves and tossed them in the trash while Shea pulled her feet down from the stirrups and sat up on the examining table. "You finished that course of antibiotic I gave you for your sinus infection?"

Shea nodded, self-consciously adjusting her paper gown over her bare knees.

"Good." The doctor picked up her pen and began making notes on the chart lying open on the short counter next to the table. "And no more headaches or fever since then?"

"No." At least the headache caused by her infection was gone. The one caused by living in the same apartment as Pax for the past two and a half weeks and pretending that it was remotely normal, though, was alive and well.

The only ones in that apartment who seemed comfortable with the situation were, strangely enough, the dog and the cat. Marsha-Marsha had finally ventured off the top of the bookshelves and was tolerating Hooch's enthusiastic curiosity where she was concerned, with only the occasional hiss and howl.

"Anything else you want to discuss before Daddy joins us again? Questions? Concerns? Trust me, Shea. There is nothing I haven't already heard over the years."

She shook her head.

The doctor looked at her over the tops of her stylish glasses as if she were deciding whether to believe her or not. But she just nodded after a moment and smiled again. "All right, then." She made another note on the chart and closed the folder. "Once you're dressed, I'll see you and Pax in my office." She slipped out the door and closed it.

Shea exhaled and quickly hopped off the examining table. Thankfully, Pax had been banished from the examining room by the nurse at the beginning of the appointment when she'd handed Shea the paper gown. Now that she was done, she pulled it off and shoved it in the small bin in the corner before dragging on her jeans. She couldn't blame it on her imagination when the zipper didn't fasten as easily as it had the week before. She wasn't showing yet. Not really. She knew, because she looked in the mirror in Pax's extra room every morning before she got dressed for work. But her pants were definitely getting tighter.

She fastened her brand-new bra, one of several she'd bought before the appointment, and yanked her sweater over her head. Then flipping her hair free of the neckline, she left the examining room and followed where the nurse was pointing to Dr. Montgomery's office.

Pax was already there, sitting in one of the chairs situated in front of the tidy desk. He barely gave her a glance when she took the chair next to him.

She wished she had the same control.

He'd come straight from the boat works to meet her at the doctor's office and was dressed in a plain white shirt rolled up to his elbows and well-worn jeans with heavy work boots. It didn't take much to envision him with a tool belt fastened around his lean hips, wielding saw and hammer. Preferably without The Shirt.

A shiver danced down her spine.

What was *wrong* with her? She'd never had lascivious thoughts this way about Bruce, and she'd thought she loved him.

"What should we be doing about her morning sickness?" Pax clearly had no problems focusing on the matter at hand. "She's up at six every day losing it."

Since she'd moved in, their exchanges had been pretty limited, mostly confined to how Pax thought she worked too many hours and wasn't sleeping and eating enough. He also couldn't understand why she insisted on keeping her ancient car when he had two perfectly good vehicles at their disposal. "How do you know that?"

He gave her a look. "We live under the same roof." He turned his attention back to the doctor, who was watching them curiously.

"As long as Shea's able to keep most of her food down during the day, I wouldn't worry," the doctor advised. "The nausea typically begins easing up now after the first trimester. And yes, I know you and Shea can pinpoint the time of conception, but the weeks of her pregnancy are counted from her last period. So officially, this is her second trimester.

"But if Shea's nausea doesn't resolve, and it becomes really severe, there are steps we'll discuss taking. In the meantime, home remedies are generally the route we go." She leaned forward and caught Shea's eyes. "And, of course, I can't emphasize enough that you should try to minimize stress as much as you can. Meditation, light exercise—"

"I'll start taking Hooch out every day for one of his walks," she offered quickly. The last thing she wanted to do was get on the topic of stress. Hers was already topping the charts; she didn't need Pax adding the subject to his arsenal.

The doctor nodded approvingly, and before Pax could start in on another question, Shea pointedly looked at the clock on the wall. She'd told Harvey she'd only be gone over her lunch break and it was well past that. She had no desire to antagonize her boss further when he was still more than a little peeved that he'd had to learn from other sources that she was living with Pax.

Now he wanted her to do a set of pieces about their supposed "big romance" and couldn't understand why she refused.

"I've already taken up plenty of your time, doctor. So if that's it, I should get back to work."

"That's it," the doctor said easily. Shea could only imagine what the woman was thinking. But these days, she was certain Dr. Montgomery saw a lot of couples who were pregnant outside of marriage. She removed a sheet of paper from Shea's chart and handed it to her. "Just give that to Maria on your way out and we'll see you again next month. And, of course, please call me if you become concerned about anything at all before then."

"Thanks." Shea took the form and hastily left the office ahead of Pax. Dr. Montgomery's practice was a busy one; there were two women ahead of Shea once she'd followed the maze of hallways to the exit and the young woman sitting behind the tall counter there. Pax reached her just as it was her turn and slid his business card across to Maria before Shea had even pulled out her own wallet.

"Make sure everything is billed there," he told the girl, who blushed a little under his easy smile and assured him she would take care of it.

"I have insurance," Shea whispered under her breath while the girl went to make a copy of the card.

"With crappy coverage, I'm betting," he countered. "I can afford it."

She pressed her lips together, wondering if he actually did know just how skimpy the policy was that she paid for through the *Tub*. She wouldn't put it past him to have called Harvey to find out. Maria returned and gave him back his card, then tapped on her computer keyboard a few times.

"We can fit you in at nine on April 10," she said. "It's the doctor's first appointment of the day, so you're less likely to get stuck with a wait like you did today."

He upped the wattage on his smile for Maria. "Can you find something later in the afternoon?" His hand slid over Shea's shoulder and squeezed. "She doesn't feel so great in the mornings."

Maria nodded eagerly, obviously charmed. She typed busily. "What about the same day at three?"

"Fine," Shea said quickly, lest Pax find something wanting about that time also, but mostly because his hand was burning on her shoulder and making her mouth dry.

The girl made out a reminder card and handed it to Pax. "See you next month." The poor thing practically had stars in her eyes.

Shea managed not to roll her own eyes and headed out the exit to the drizzly day. Pax quickly caught up with her, obviously intent on walking her to her car considering the hand he wrapped around her elbow.

She wasn't sure if that was easier or harder to ignore

than having his hand on her shoulder. Probably because she couldn't forget what it felt like to have his hands *all* over her. Fortunately, she'd gotten a decent parking spot, so the torment wouldn't have to last long.

"Erik and I have a client dinner tonight," he said. "I'd like you to come with me."

She almost tripped over her feet. "Why?"

"Because both Erik and our client, Miles White, are bringing their wives," he said smoothly, as if that explained it all.

She opened her mouth to say no. She really did. What was the point of behaving like the couple that they weren't? "Okay."

The corners of his lips kicked up slightly and she looked away, shoving her hand into her voluminous purse in search of her keys as she crossed the last few feet to the car.

"And tell Harvey you need a few hours off tomorrow."

She found the keys and closed her fingers around them so tightly it hurt. "I have a busy schedule," she said quickly. "I'm going to Kirkland for a park dedication and then afterward have to head over to a high school that's conducting a fashion show. The students in Home Ec made the clothes out of recycled materials."

"That's not going to take you all day. When's the park thing?"

She couldn't make herself lie, much as it appealed. She stifled a sigh and pulled out the keys. "After lunch."

He slipped the keys out of her grasp and unlocked her car door for her. "Then we'll meet the Realtor in the morning. He's found a few houses that look promising."

"You're really looking at houses?" She hadn't believed he was serious when he'd mentioned it that one time, and it hadn't come up since.

"I really am." He opened the door. "And I want your opinion."

"Why?"

He angled his head, watching her. "Because it matters to me."

Her chest squeezed. She was getting in deeper and deeper and she wasn't sure how she'd ever get out.

Or if she wanted to.

And that scared her most of all.

"Fine," she said brusquely and slid into the car. "But I have to be done by eleven." She yanked the door shut and shakily fit the key into the ignition.

Instead of moving away from the vehicle, he knocked on the window and waited until she rolled it down. "Now what?"

"Reservations tonight are at seven. Dressy." His eyes were amused, his voice bland. "Because I know how preoccupied you get over what to wear."

"I do not," she denied testily. She hated worrying about what to wear and he darned well knew it. She turned the car key. The engine clicked once, gave a groan and went silent.

Great. Just…great.

She pulled out the key and looked at Pax again.

"This wouldn't happen if you drove my car," he pointed out, the smooth soul of reason.

She ignored him, rolled up the window and got back out of the car, dragging her purse and computer case along. "Will you drop me off or not?"

"Since you asked so nicely."

She turned her face up to him, letting the faint drizzle cool her skin. The last time they'd stood like this together on a wet, gray day had been on the deck of *Honey Girl*.

And thinking about *that* didn't slow the blood zipping around in her veins at all. "Please."

In answer, he took the strap of her computer case. "I'll send someone over to get the car."

He'd take care of everything for her if she let him. "I can do it."

"I know you can. But you don't have to. You're the one who's pregnant. So let me do this."

There was no point in arguing. And the truth was that she was heartily tired of dealing with the darned car. "Fine. Thank you." She hitched her purse over her shoulder and slammed the door shut before walking to the trunk and opening it. The last time she'd had the car at the mechanic after the ice storm, it had been there for nearly two weeks. She needed to make sure she had everything she needed.

"What's that?" Pax tried to looked past her at the shopping bag in the trunk, but she grabbed it before he could.

"I bought a few things on my way over here."

He lifted an eyebrow. The devilish look in his eyes would have made an angel jump ship. "From *Victoria's Secret*? Anything you intend to share?"

Her cheeks felt hot. She closed the trunk and turned to his SUV parked in the next row. "Don't think they'd fit you," she returned. "But interesting to learn you've got a thing for wearing women's underwear." She had no desire to tell him she'd gone in search of new bras because the ones she already had were now unbearably snug.

His soft laughter followed her. "Just a thing for getting a certain woman out of hers."

She shot him a look over her shoulder. "Very funny."

"I thought so."

She exhaled and quickened her step, for all the good it did her. His long legs would always outpace hers. When they reached the SUV, he opened the door for her and she stuck her purse and bag on the seat. And even though she was prepared, when he closed his hands around her hips and helped her up, she still went hot inside.

She couldn't bring herself to look at him, so she busied herself with the computer case he'd handed over, pulling out a pad of notes she'd been making on her assignments for that week and pretending to study it while he drove her to her work. She didn't put it away until he pulled to a stop on the street in front of the building.

"I'll pick you up at four."

"I can take the…" The words died on her lips. He'd definitely argue with her over public transportation. "Thanks. I need to go by and see Cornelia today, too." It wasn't Shea's usual day, but Cornelia had needed to reschedule. Shea'd finished reading every one of the letters Cornelia had given her and hadn't found a single idea worth pursuing, but she still needed to return them.

"No problem."

Aware of the traffic piling up behind them, she gathered her stuff and got out. "I'll see you in a few hours."

"Say hi to Harv. Tell him we'll have him over for dinner sometime."

She rolled her eyes, knowing he was joking. "He'd wet his pants." A car horn tooted behind them, so she quickly closed the door and walked to the sidewalk. Pax continued on and the traffic churned along behind him.

Only when she could no longer see his taillights did she finally turn and go inside.

She took the elevator up to the *Tub*'s floor, where everything was as chaotic as it usually was during the last few hours of their workday. Her desk wasn't much more than a cubbyhole in a back corner, and though she didn't particularly want to pass by the glass window of Harvey's office to get there, she couldn't avoid it.

Fortunately, he was hunched at his desk, clearly intent on something else as she scurried past. She dumped her stuff on the floor next to her desk and sat down to get to work. She was already late getting an article in that he'd wanted that morning. She had been too busy hiding out in the ladies' room, losing her breakfast for the umpteenth time, to finish it before she'd left for her appointment.

It was nearly four when she finally was satisfied with the piece. She emailed it to Harvey and then looked over the wall of her cubby to Josh Cooper, who was the only one left besides her who hadn't deserted the place for the day. "He's been really quiet in there this afternoon."

Josh nodded his prematurely balding head. "Sometimes miracles do happen." He looked up from his computer across at her. "But that's the stuff you get to write about. Not me." He looked back at his screen again. "Nothing but corruption and greed, death and dying for me," he muttered.

Shea stared. Then shook herself. No way would Josh want to trade seats with her. "Not many miracles," she said, pushing out of her seat. "But I did get to interview that duck living in the school fountain." She walked across the room to Harvey's door and stuck her head in. "I just—" Her words jammed in her throat.

Harvey wasn't sitting at his desk.

He was lying collapsed on the floor behind it.

Panic roared through her. "Call 911," she yelled to Josh, raced around the desk and kneeled in the tight space beside her boss.

"Harvey? Can you hear me?" She shook his beefy shoulder, but he didn't move. She bent low, racking her brains to remember the CPR class she'd taken years ago. She couldn't feel even a wisp of breath on her cheek.

"Come on, Harvey," she begged. "You're too ornery

for this. *Cooper!*" She stacked her hands on the center of Harvey's chest and pressed down with the heel of her palm. Pressed hard. Pressed fast. Something about a hundred compressions a minute hovered in her brain. "Josh!"

He practically skidded into the room, his eyes wide. "Jesus." He had his phone clutched to his ear. "What's wrong with him?"

"How should I know? Heart attack?" She kept counting compressions in her head. She could barely feel Harvey's chest giving beneath her pushing and she leaned farther on her knees, putting all of her weight behind it. "Is somebody coming or not?"

"Yeah." He listened at the phone and kneeled beside her. "They want to know if you're experienced at CPR."

"Do I *look* experienced?" She stopped and leaned over Harvey again, desperately wanting to hear or feel a breath but getting nothing. "Are you?"

"Hell, no." He listened again. "We're just supposed to do the chest compressions," he said and nudged her aside. "Take the phone. I'll help." He shoved it into her hands.

She shakily put the cell phone to her ear. Her heart was pounding from anxiety and exertion. "Hello? Please tell me you've sent an ambulance or something."

"They're already on their way, ma'am," the 911 operator assured her. "Is the patient still unconscious?"

"Yes." She hit the speaker button and dropped the phone on the desk beside them. "Can you still hear me?"

"Yes, ma'am. Do you know how old the patient is?"

"*Harvey,*" she said sharply. "His name is Harvey Hightower."

"I'm sorry," the operator's voice was calm. "Do you know Harvey's age? Approximate age?"

"Sixty-one," she said. Josh was huffing even worse than she'd been from the effort of doing the chest compressions, and she waved him off before he ended up lying on the floor next to their boss. He moved his hands and she immediately replaced them with hers.

"Ma'am?" The phone crackled a little. "The paramedics are arriving on the scene now. If someone there would make certain they have access—"

"On it." Josh pushed to his feet and ran out of the office, obviously all too glad for the escape.

Shea didn't look away from Harvey's face. It was drained of all its usual ruddiness. "Come on, Harvey," she said breathlessly between compressions. "Give me a little help here." She pumped with all of her might, huffing her hair out of her face. "Pax says...you should come for...dinner!" She heard footsteps running outside the office and looked over, expecting to see the paramedics.

But it was Pax, his dark eyes nearly black and his face pale. "I saw the paramedics outside," he said roughly.

She'd been holding it together until then. But for some reason, the sight of him made everything inside her start to unravel. "He's not breathing," she cried.

He peeled off his leather jacket and tossed it aside. There wasn't much room in the tight confines, but he solved that problem easily enough by grabbing the big man beneath his shoulders and dragging him around the desk. She scrambled along, trying to keep up the compressions. Her arms and shoulders were starting to ache. Pax moved her out of the way and took over.

She fell back on her heels, breathing hard. "How'd you beat the paramedics up here?"

"They were still unloading stuff. I took the stairs because they'd already commandeered the elevator." He looked at her. "I thought something happened to you."

She was shivering and, without thinking, she pulled his jacket over her shoulders. It was warm and smelled of him. "There are twenty other offices in this building, most with more employees than the *Washtub!*" Why would he automatically single her out?

"And only one of you."

She was still trying to absorb that when they heard a clatter and looked up to see the emergency team arriving, gurney and all.

"We've got it now, sir," the one in the lead said.

Pax immediately moved aside and held out his hand to help her to her feet. He pulled her out of the office and when he would have let her hand go again, she curled her fingers, keeping hold. She looked toward the elevator, but there was no sign of Josh.

"How well do you know the patient?" the medic standing outside the office doorway asked. He was obviously the one in charge of the details while the other three crowded around Harvey on the floor.

"I've worked for him for six years." She gnawed the inside of her cheek, looking past him to the others. They'd pulled open Harvey's shirt and were working rapidly. "He's going to be okay, right?"

"We're all doing our best to see that he is." He wore a radio clipped near his collar and he spoke into it, relaying the vitals that his associates were calling out. A moment later, he was focused on Shea again. "Do you know what he was doing before he collapsed?"

She pinched her nose and shook her head. "He was sitting at his desk as usual around two." After that, she'd been focused on her writing. "I should have heard something." She looked at Pax. "Somebody should have heard something! He could have been lying there like that for two minutes or two hours!"

"The important thing is that you rendered aid when you did find him," the detail guy said, bringing her focus back to him. "Does Mr. Hightower have any medical history that you know about?"

She shook her head. "He's worked here every day of every week since I've been here. I've never even seen him sick."

"Wife? Other family members we can notify?"

"No." She clasped Pax's coat more tightly with her fist. "I think he was married once, but it was over a long time ago."

"And you don't know of any other emergency contact?"

She bit her lip and shook her head. "I'm sorry. I just don't know. We only talked about work."

"What about on his payroll record?" Pax suggested.

"Harvey was the payroll record," Josh said, finally reappearing. "He was the only one keeping this place going."

Shea frowned. "The publisher—"

"—pulled the plug two months ago. Just couldn't keep up against the internet anymore. Especially a small outfit like this. Profits were nonexistent for too long."

"But he never said!" Bewildered, she looked again at Harvey lying prone on his office floor. Pax's arm slid around her shoulder and he held her tight. "Nothing's changed around here. He hasn't let anyone go, nothing. How did you know, Josh? Did he tell you?"

"I came in late one night to run some background information and overheard him on the phone in his office. He obviously wanted it kept confidential that he was looking for other backers." He shrugged. "Stress must've been too much."

"Ready to transport."

Pax nudged her to one side while the medics maneuvered the gurney closer to the doorway and loaded Harvey onto it. One was squeezing a breathing apparatus over Harvey's mouth as they jogged with the gurney to the elevator.

"Where are you taking him?" Pax called after them.

"Virginia Mason," the detail man informed as they stepped onto the elevator. The doors closed with a ding, and just that quickly, they were gone, the *Washtub* offices surreally quiet.

Josh retrieved his phone from Harvey's desk.

"What took you so long to get back up here?" Shea asked him.

"Had to take the stairs. They'd locked the elevator on this floor. Probably so they wouldn't get stuck waiting for it when they needed to leave." He looked around at the disarray in Harvey's office and sighed a little.

"The *Tub*'s really going under?" Harvey's whole life was the paper.

"It's what I heard." He pocketed his phone and went to his cube to retrieve the backpack he used as a briefcase. "If you're smart," he advised on his way to the elevator, "you'll start spiffing up your résumé, too, and get it out there same as me."

The last thing she was thinking about was her job.

"What an ass," Pax said the second he was gone. He pulled her close and kissed her forehead, his arms wrapping around her as she stood there shivering in his coat. "We'll drive over to the hospital," he promised without even needing to be asked. "And we'll stay until we know he's going to be okay."

If he was going to be okay.

Her eyes burned and she let her head rest weakly against Pax's chest. His warmth penetrated, strong and steady, and something—relief, comfort, peace—rolled through her. "What about the dinner with Erik and your client?"

"Erik'll handle it. No worries there." His arms tightened. "You're going to be at the hospital with Harvey. And

I'm going to be at the hospital with you. I'm not going to leave you."

She closed her eyes tightly. *Ever?* But the word didn't make it past her lips and more quickly than she was ready for, he'd moved her away from him.

"Where's your desk?"

She gestured. "Corner."

He walked over and saw the shopping bag sitting on the floor. He grabbed it, along with her purse and jacket. "Anything else?"

"Laptop. And that big manila envelope on the shelf is for Cornelia." She didn't know what was wrong with her, not going and getting her own things. It was just too easy to let him take care of it. Which he did more than competently. He slung the laptop bag over his shoulder, right along with the purse strap and the shopping bag into which he dumped Cornelia's collection of letters. Then he tucked her shoulders under his other arm and walked back to the elevator.

"Nothing to lock up, I take it."

She shook her head and pushed the call button. "Security guards are on duty downstairs during off-hours. " She looked up at Pax and laughed brokenly. "Just this morning Harvey was yelling and threatening to fire us all. Same as he's done nearly every day I've worked here. He never said a word. Not a single word about what was happening. And Josh knew."

"Guy's a tool," Pax muttered and ushered her onto the empty car when the doors finally slid open.

"Because he didn't break Harvey's confidence?"

"Because he cares more about his damn résumé than a man's life."

She leaned against him. "Harvey doesn't even have any family. There's nobody to call." The emptiness of it horrified her. She looked up at Pax. "Nobody to worry about him. Miss him."

He cupped her face. "Yes, he does." He kissed her forehead. "He has you." He smiled a little, his eyes like warm chocolate. "Cupcake."

She chewed the inside of her lip. Her nose burned and her eyes tingled. "If he makes it through this, he can call me that all he wants." She swiped her cheeks and stepped back when the elevator reached the ground floor. "It's silly, you know," she murmured as they quickly crossed the lobby, "but aside from my mother, he's the only one who's been in my life for more than a handful of years."

"She married seven times, right? That kind of turnover doesn't allow much time to get to know someone, I imagine."

"No. The longest she was with any of them so far was two and a half years. That was with Ruben, and that's counting both times they were married. If she sticks with Jonathan, though, she might beat that." She studied Pax for a moment. He was still in the same clothes he'd had on earlier, though it seemed as if days had passed since then, rather than mere hours. "Come July, I'll have known *you* for three years."

He pushed open the lobby door and waited for her to pass through. "Independence Day," he agreed. "At the Red, White and Blue Regatta."

"Which you and *Honey Girl* won." She remembered the day as if it were yesterday. He'd been as bright and shining as the sun, and looking at him with his arms around the two stunning women who'd been part of his sailing crew had just made Bruce's recent jilting feel that much more acute. But Harvey had sent her with specific instructions to get a story from Pax, and so she had.

Strange how she could recall the details of that day so

clearly when she could barely recall the details of the day her fiancé had dumped her.

"So where does that put me in the lineup of years?" Pax asked.

She pressed her tongue to the back of her teeth, gathering herself. She wondered why she'd never realized it before. "Second, actually."

"Much as I always like to be first," he gave her a faint wink, "I'll concede the spot to Harvey for now. Now let's get to the hospital and see how he's doing."

Chapter Twelve

When they arrived at the hospital, they soon learned that Harvey was in surgery, undergoing an emergency bypass, and nobody would be allowed to see him for some time.

Which gave Pax all the excuse he needed to get Shea to go to the cafeteria and eat something. It was still early in the evening, even though it felt like the middle of the night with everything that had gone on. The place was busy with staffers and visitors alike working their way through the lines with their trays. He spotted a small, un-occupied table and sat Shea down. She was still wearing his coat wrapped around her like a blanket and her eyes were huge in her pale face. He wanted to take her home and put her safely to bed, but he knew there was no chance of that happening.

He asked her what she thought she could stand to eat, and went to join the line. He'd called and spoken with Cornelia already and had sent a text message to his partner about the situation, but while he was waiting, he took out his phone again and made a quick call to Erik. Just as Pax had known he would, his partner had his back. He also offered to cancel the dinner meeting altogether and come to the hospital. He and Rory already had a babysitter for Tyler and they could come to sit with them while they waited for news on Harvey, but Pax told him not to. "I want to get Shea home as soon as I can," he said.

"Right." Erik understood that completely, possessing a healthy protective streak for his own new family. "Update me when you can."

Pax pocketed his phone and moved along with the line, collecting the soup Shea had requested and adding an oversized club sandwich for himself. He bought a small bottle of milk and a large coffee and carried everything back to the table where she was waiting.

Her gaze immediately latched onto the coffee.

"No," he said and pointedly moved it closer to him. "You had coffee this morning already." She'd brewed a pot before taking her shower. He'd sat there drinking it, wondering what secret she and the women over at Cornelia's place possessed that made it taste twice as good as anything he made. But mostly what he'd really wanted to do was join Shea in the shower.

The same way he'd wanted to every morning since she'd moved in.

She was giving him a look that was half consternation and half pout. "I just want a sip."

"I'll pour some in your milk then. Maybe you'll actually drink it for once." She generally ignored the milk bottle in their refrigerator, though he'd discovered that she could go through fresh fruit juice like a freight train.

"I don't want coffee in my milk," she argued. "I want milk in my coffee. There is a difference, you know." But she peeled back the foil seal beneath the cap and nudged the short bottle toward him.

"You need to drink some plain first or there's no room to add the coffee."

She made a face. "I hate plain milk."

So did he, but he wasn't going to admit that right now. "Think about little Fig Newton then." The doctor had told them the baby was about the size of a large fig and as he'd hoped, Shea's expression lightened a little.

"A fig," she murmured, holding up her thumb and forefinger about two inches apart. "Amazing there's someone growing inside me who is only this big."

He slid the soup in front of her. "You want him to be bigger already?"

"Good grief, not yet." She picked up her spoon and dipped it into the bowl. "My pants are already too tight and I just blew Cornelia's last paycheck on a bunch of bras." She shot him a chagrined look as if she hadn't expected to admit that.

"So that's what the Victoria's Secret bag was about."

She looked back at her soup bowl and lifted her shoulder. "About a month overdue," she murmured. "First thing that happened was my boobs got even bigger."

He couldn't help it. "You say that like it's a bad thing."

Her eyebrow lifted and she made a face. "Spoken like a man who doesn't have to cart around cantaloupes all the time."

He grinned. "Not cantaloupes," he corrected. "More like really, *really* perfect grapefruit."

"I'm just a regular fruit salad here," she said dryly. But her eyes had lightened a little more.

"Women still have it easier than men," he went on.

She made a skeptical sound. "Please. In what world are *you* living?"

He unwrapped the sandwich and set a quarter of it on a napkin in front of her. "Seriously." He waved his hand. "You all are able to keep what you're feeling about certain matters a complete mystery while us poor slobs are standing out at attention announcing it."

She gave him a deadpan look, though her eyes glinted with sharp humor. "Want to give away that particular ability?"

"Hell, no."

Her lips curved wryly. "Didn't think so. Consider it fair exchange for the pleasures women endure being pregnant with men's babies."

He'd had plenty of pleasure making her that way, even as unintentional as it had been. "Are you sorry? About being pregnant?" The question came out without his thinking about it.

Her eyes softened. She shook her head. "I'm getting used to the idea of Fig Newton."

And *him?* Was she getting used to the idea of him?

If things had gone according to plan, he'd have found out the answer to that for certain after dinner tonight. He'd intended to propose then.

Properly. So she'd understand he really meant it.

He'd even found a ring. One that matched the color of her eyes.

And if she turns you down again? What then?

"Newton Merrick," he mused, focusing instead on what was, instead of what might not ever be.

She made a face. "Oh, that sounds just horrible."

"It worked for Sir Isaac. But then again, Newton was his last name. For our child, everyone would probably shorten it to Newt. There've been some famous Newts."

She made a reluctant sound. "Yes, but—"

"Well, we've got another twenty-some weeks to figure it out."

"That doesn't sound very far off, does it?"

"Not so much," he agreed. He took the lid off the steaming coffee and poured a small measure inside the milk bottle.

She immediately put down her spoon and put the cap on the milk, shook it once, uncapped it and greedily tilted it to her lips.

"That is the way I first learned to drink coffee. My father would sneak a shot or two of coffee into Bea's and my milk glasses when Mom wasn't looking."

"I was drinking it straight up by the time I was fifteen." She held out the bottle. "Little more? Please? Pretty please with sugar on top?"

He deliberately put the lid back on the coffee cup and took a drink.

She huffed and set the milk bottle down, picking up the portion of sandwich he'd given her. "One of these days, I'm going to dangle something right in front of you that you desperately want and not give you any at all," she warned.

He let out an abrupt laugh directed right at himself. "Sweetheart, that boat's already sailed out farther than you know."

She clearly missed his implication, though.

For a woman who wrote some of the cleverest things he'd ever read, she was nevertheless stunningly unaware of a lot.

"Once you finish your food," he suggested, "we'll go check on Harvey."

"Pax."

The nerves at the base of his spine tightened. "Yeah?"

"Thanks for being here."

"I said I would be."

"I know." She chewed the corner of her lip for a moment. "But, still. Thanks. I'm…I'm really glad."

"So am I, Shea. So am I."

Harvey's bypass turned out to be a triple. And though Pax's intention had been to get Shea home as soon as he could, the longer Harvey's surgery went on, he'd had to settle for getting her to put her feet up in the surgical waiting room. Only one other couple had been there, and the couches and chairs were plentiful, so she'd finally stretched out on one and curled her arm under her head and closed her eyes.

She hadn't slept though. He could tell.

Finally, shortly before midnight, an unfamiliar doctor came to let them know that Harvey was out of surgery and in recovery. It would be hours yet before he'd be up for even the briefest of visits.

"But he's going to be okay," Shea persisted. "He'll make a complete recovery?"

"No reason why he shouldn't have his normal life," the doctor assured her. He was aware that they weren't related to Harvey and, in the absence of any immediate family, probably gave them more information than was usual. "As long as he makes a few necessary lifestyle changes." He patted Shea's arm. "The nurse will tell him that you were here waiting for him. But you should go home. Get some rest. You can see him tomorrow. And he can thank you, himself, for saving his life." He gave them a tired smile and left the waiting room.

"You heard him." Pax said. "Time to go home."

"What kind of a normal life is Harvey going to have," she whispered, "with the *Washtub* going under?"

"I don't know. But that's not something you need to worry about tonight." He grabbed her purse and their jackets and steered her out of the waiting room. "Tonight, you can go to sleep knowing he's going to see another sunrise."

"And I didn't save his life," she demurred. "The surgeons did that."

"Only because he wasn't already dead," he countered bluntly. She looked hollow-eyed and exhausted and it took considerable effort not to push her into one of the wheelchairs that they passed in the corridors and roll her out to the parking lot. But she kept plugging along, and finally they reached his SUV and he drove them home.

Hooch was waiting with a slathering tongue for Shea when they walked through the door, and Pax left them to it while he turned off the security system and went into the extra bedroom she was using. He dumped her belongings on the neatly made bed there.

When he returned, he found her sitting at the counter in the darkened kitchen, looking out at the city lights. "So where are these houses you want to see?" Her voice was soft.

"One's in the Queen Anne district."

She looked at him, but the room was too dark to read her expression. "Pricey," she murmured.

"Yeah. But it's near one of the best private schools in the area."

"Brandlebury Academy? Isn't that a little…excessive? And premature, considering he's not even born yet?"

"Never too early to think about stuff like that." He'd always been skeptical when he'd heard others say it, but now that he and Shea had a son coming, he finally understood. "And the other house is in Magnolia."

At that, she visibly stiffened.

"Is it the fact that my grandparents live there that bothers you, or the fact that your mother does?" he asked.

She was silent for a moment. "I guess that's probably not difficult information to uncover."

Not at all. He'd simply asked Cornelia when he'd called her from the hospital. "Would have been easier if you ever offered any information regarding your mother."

"You know enough."

"I know the seven marriages bit," he allowed. "Have you told her about—" he almost said *us* "—the baby?"

She shook her head. "She won't welcome the news the way your parents did."

"Why?"

"Because it's just one more sign that she's getting older. Because it's just one more piece of proof that I'm exactly like her." She rubbed her hands down her thighs and sighed. "Doomed to repeat all of her worst mistakes."

"Why do you care? You know it's not true."

"Do I?" She stood. "I don't want to talk about her, Pax. Okay? I'll tell her. Obviously, I'll tell her. Just not—" She shook her head. "Not yet."

"Is that the real reason you don't want to marry me? Is it less about the baby and more about proving you're not like her?"

"Pax."

"I'm just trying to understand, Shea."

"The only thing to understand is that marriages don't last." She raised her palm to cut off his obvious objection. "The various other Merrick and Mahoney unions excluded."

"You used to say it was relationships that didn't last. That you didn't believe in them."

"Relationships. Marriages. What's the difference? Is there one without the other?"

"What about love?"

She went still. She didn't look at him. "I'm exhausted,"

she finally said and started to leave the room. "I'm going to go to bed."

"I never took you for a coward before, Shea."

She stopped.

"What are you afraid will happen if you just let yourself care about someone?"

"I'll find him collapsed on the floor in his office," she said huskily. She looked over her shoulder at Pax, and from the faint light from the bedroom down the hall, he could see the shimmer in her eyes. "I'll let myself believe and trust." She took a quick breath. "And *need,* and when it blows up in my face again, where will I be? Alone. And broken."

"So you'd rather not try. Not let yourself." He walked closer, leaning toward her. "You'd rather be a woman who ends up like Harvey?"

She winced. "I'm *not* going to be like Harvey either. Because we're having a baby. I'll be a mother. Always."

"And do you want to raise our son believing what you believe?" He cupped her cheek in his hand. "You want Fig so afraid of his own emotions that the first time he meets a girl who knocks him for a loop he runs the other direction?"

She sniffled. "No!"

"How's he going to learn otherwise? You learned what you believe at your mother's knee, sweetheart."

She dashed her hand across her cheek. "He won't have just my knee. He'll have yours, too."

"Thought you believed I wouldn't stick around for the long haul."

After a moment, she said softly, "I was wrong. I think you'll be there for your son always."

His chest ached. "And for you?"

She looked away. "I think you deserve someone who believes in the same things you believe."

"Not someone I love?"

"Pax."

"Come on, Shea." Maybe it was the long day taking its toll. Maybe it was the weather or the moon or the city lights twinkling in the window behind her or the fact that he was just plain tired of the pretense.

Maybe it was the fact that his plans were blowing all to hell, and he didn't know what else to do.

"You have to know by now how I feel about you!"

"Responsible," she returned. "You feel responsible because I'm pregnant!"

"Hell, yes, I feel responsible!" He grabbed her arm and tugged her around to face him, pressing his palm flat against her abdomen. "Fig is my child. You're his mother. But he wouldn't exist at all if I hadn't been freaking crazy for *you* to begin with."

"And I don't want to end up hurting you because *you're* his father!" She was breathing fast. "I never said we didn't have…chemistry. Good, Lord. I'm the one who—" she broke off. "That day on *Honey Girl,* I'm the one who came on to you. I know that. But chemistry—"

"Passion."

"Fine! Passion! That doesn't equal love either!"

"No. Love to you is a guy who promises to marry you and leaves you at the altar," he said flatly. "Is that right? Are you still in love with *that* jackass?"

She pushed him away. "Don't."

"Is he the one you dream about?" He followed her out of the kitchen. "Long for when you're all alone?"

She rounded on him, throwing her arms wide. "What do you want from me, Pax?"

He wanted everything from her. But he realized that,

even more, he wanted everything *for* her. "I want you to believe that you deserve more." His voice sounded as raw as his throat felt.

"And if it's not you?"

He wondered if the pain inside his chest was the kind of pain Harvey had felt.

"Then it's not me. But at least there would be someone," he said quietly. He looked past her to the light shining from her room. "Go to bed. You need to get some sleep." Then he picked up his keys that he'd left on the hall table.

"Where are you going?"

"I'll bunk down on *Honey Girl.*" She'd been his first love and she was always waiting. Willing and ready for anything he put her through. "I have her moored at the boat works. Keys to the Audi are on the dresser in my room."

She made a sound. "This is your home. You shouldn't have to go somewhere else."

He didn't have to. But he wasn't sure that he didn't need to. If only for his own sanity. "If you don't want to drive her, then call me in the morning." He jabbed in the code on the security panel because Shea was forever forgetting to set it herself, then pulled open the door. "I'll pick you up and take you to the hospital."

"*I* don't want you to go." Her husky voice followed him. "You're the one who's in my dreams, Pax." She darted around him until she was standing in his path. One hundred and eleven pounds—according to Dr. Montgomery's nurse that morning—of curvy, short female blocking him in.

"The only one in my dreams," she added. "And I don't want you to leave." She stared into his face. "I'm *asking* you not to leave. Not…not tonight."

"Because you're upset about Harvey."

"Because I'm afraid if you go, you won't come back," she whispered.

He let out a long, slow breath. Looking at her was a physical pain. But he took a step back through the doorway. She followed and pushed it closed. "Thank you."

"I don't want your thanks, Shea." He wanted her heart, and he was honestly unsure whether she'd ever let herself give it. He dropped the keys on the table again and went into his bedroom. He pushed the door closed, pinching the bridge of his nose for a long, long moment. Then he wearily pulled off his clothes and went into the bathroom to shower off the day. Rinsing away the reality, though, wasn't so easily done.

He toweled off roughly and yanked back the covers on his bed. But a soft scratch and whine on his door stopped him from hitting the sheets. He went to the door and pulled it open. "Come on in, Hooch," he murmured.

The dog trotted in and jumped on the foot of his bed. He started to close the door again but a hand stopped him. "What about me?" Shea asked hesitantly from the other side. "Can I come in, too?"

His grip tightened around the door handle. "The rule still stands, Shea. Come in only if you're going to stay."

She nudged the door open a little wider and slipped through. She was still in her jeans and long-sleeved T-shirt and he heard her suck in a breath when she looked at him. He hadn't bothered to turn on a bedroom light, but the one in the bathroom was still on.

He was still mostly wet from the shower and as naked as it got.

"Still sure?"

Her gaze flicked from him to the bed, where the white sheets looked ghostly pale in the dim light, and back again. Then she moistened her lips and walked across the room to the blinds that were wide open at the window. "Do you mind?"

He liked the view of the sky outside, but he was willing to let her desire for a little more privacy prevail. "No."

She adjusted them slightly, obscuring the view from outside but not closing them entirely. Then she turned and faced him, and with a complete economy of effort, pulled off her clothes and dropped them as haphazardly on the floor as he'd done with his own. Her long hair flowed over her shoulders and down her spine as she padded barefoot past him and knelt on the bed. "Do I look sure enough for you?"

He exhaled roughly and snapped his fingers at the dog. "Go to your own bed, Hooch."

The dog huffed but obediently jumped off the bed and trotted back out the bedroom door.

Pax walked over to her and reached out, sliding her long, silky hair behind her shoulders. Her skin was as creamy smooth as it had been in December and her hips just as narrow. But her breasts were fuller, the tight crests a darker rose.

And this time, when he pressed his palm against her abdomen, with nothing between them but skin, he could feel a soft curving there that hadn't been noticeable before.

She made a soft sound and rose on her knees, urging his hand lower as her mouth found his. "Touch me," she whispered against his lips. "Not just Fig."

His pulse roared in his head and he slid his hand between her legs, where she was as warm and wet as he remembered in his dreams. He sucked in a breath that tasted of hers and she gasped softly, rocking against his fingers.

She pulled his other hand to her breast. "There, too," she whispered and shuddered when he dragged his thumb over her tightly beaded nipple.

"They're not too sensitive?" He'd been doing his reading about pregnancy. About the changes going on in her body.

"Yes." She twisted one hand in his hair and closed her other boldly around him. "And if you stop, I'll lose my mind."

He'd already lost his. The second she rubbed her thumb over his head and started stroking, he was gone.

He tipped her onto her back, replacing his hand on her breast with his lips and sliding his hands beneath her thighs, dragging her to the edge of the bed and burying himself inside of her.

Her back bowed sharply and she cried out, but when he started to pull back, she twined her legs around his and moved with him.

Pleasure, deeper than anything he'd ever known, drilled straight down his spine to his very soul. She threw her arms over her head, arching harder against him and he slid his palms against hers, their fingers twining.

"Please, please." Her mouth was open, her hair tangling around them both as her hips pulsed against his, her body the sweetest glove that had ever existed. "Don't stop."

He couldn't even if he wanted to.

He pressed deeper and her fingertips curled tightly as she gasped his name. He felt ripples work through her entire body to her very center and the whirlwind was too strong to resist. His head fell to her shoulder and he mindlessly emptied himself into the storm.

And later, when the clutching little spasms inside her finally stilled and their tightly clenched hands went lax, he pulled her head onto his chest and they finally, finally slept.

Chapter Thirteen

Sunlight was streaming through the angled slats of the window blind when Shea finally opened her eyes.

She was in Pax's bed.

But he was gone.

She stretched out her arm and smoothed her palm over the pillow that still had an indentation from his head. She didn't know what would change by making love. Didn't know if anything could change.

Sighing, she rolled over and pressed her face to his pillow.

She just knew that she couldn't regret it.

"You awake in there?"

She lifted her head.

Pax was standing in the doorway, a towel wrapped low around his hips, and when she finally managed to drag her eyes away from the hard plane of his abdomen to look up at his face, he was grinning faintly.

She flushed from her head right down to her toes.

"*Now* you're shy?" He dropped the towel and climbed into bed beside her. "Turn over."

She was glad to. At least she didn't have to look at that knowing expression of his.

He slid his arm over her waist and pulled her back against him.

"Oh." She sighed softly.

"Oh." He kissed her shoulder and tucked her rear even closer against him. "How're you feeling?"

Completely wanton. "Fine. And—" she tried to ignore the way his palm was gliding down her hip "—you?"

His erection prodded her backside. "Better than I have in a long, long while."

A shiver skittered down her spine. "What time is it?"

"Nearly eight." His fingers inched down the front of her thigh. "Harvey's sleeping comfortably, according to the nurse I just spoke with."

"I should get over there."

"You've got time."

"I still have to—oh—" She exhaled shakily when his hand slid purposefully between her legs. "To go to Kirkland…Park."

"Still going to do the stories even knowing the *Tub*'s not going to make it?"

She twisted her hand in the sheet, staring blindly at the rays of sunlight on the gleaming wood floor. "I refuse to believe it's a lost cause." Her voice rose to a squeak when his fingers delved and dipped inside so, so briefly, only to circle and press and dip again.

"Well, I understand that," he murmured, kissing her shoulder again, then the curve of her neck, just below her ear. "I love the way you feel." The pulse of his heart beat against her back. "Slide your leg up."

She did, and just that perfectly, he slid inside her.

She let out a low moan.

"And I love the way you sound when I do that." His voice dropped and he rocked into her, his fingers still circling. "Do you really dream about me?"

"Yes." She arched back against him, wanting him deeper. Harder. She reached behind him and dug her fingers into his hard, muscular thigh.

"What do you dream?"

She was no more capable of hiding the truth than she was capable of hiding the fact that she was already on the verge of spiraling into oblivion. "About this. About you doing this," she gasped. "Again." She quivered. "And again and again."

His breath roughened but his hands remained gentle, his pulsing into her a seductive lullaby. Her eyes burned and she slid her hand over his, pressing his palm harder against her. Last night her body had felt split in half by him, but now, it was her heart that felt like it was being cleaved in two.

"Not everything needs to be a gale," he murmured, shifting them both until she was on her back and he was rocking gently once more in the cradle of her hips. "Sometimes it can just be a dream come true."

Tears slid from her eyes.

He circled her head with his palms and softly kissed her lips. Then one cheek. And the other. Kissing away her tears. "Everything's going to work out, Shea. Just let yourself believe. A little bit. And it will all be all right."

She couldn't answer. The words were stopped in her chest by a wall that seemed put there before she'd ever even existed. She stared into his eyes. "I'm afraid."

He lowered his forehead against hers for a moment. "I

know, sweetheart. So I won't be." He kissed her again. "I love you, Shea."

She trembled. Fresh tears fell.

"And I'm going to keep loving you until you're not afraid." He kissed her again. "And I'll still love you after that." Then he slid his hands beneath her hips, tilting her, and rocked into the very center of her being.

And even though she cracked in half and crumbled into heartbreakingly sweet pleasure, he was there, putting the pieces back together and taking her there again before finally letting himself go.

Two hours later, showered and dressed and trying to pretend that the foundations of the world she'd believed in weren't in danger of failing completely, Shea peeked her head around the curtain sectioning off Harvey's bed from the others in the unit. "Knock knock."

The back of his bed was elevated slightly and he had wires and tubes sprouting from a dozen places, but her boss still managed to give her his usual, narrow-eyed glare. "Cupcake's here," he rasped.

She smiled and walked closer to his bed, holding the stack of newspapers she had for him at an angle so he could see them before she set them on the rolling table next to his bed. "News of the world since I know you'd rather put a gun to your head than watch the television news. Brace yourself. I'm gonna kiss your cheek."

He made a low, grumbling sound. But he didn't bark at her not to. She pecked his bristly cheek, then pulled the plain chair from outside the curtain around to his bedside and sat down. He was already slowly reaching for the newspaper on the top of the stack.

"*Wall Street Journal*." He set it on the blanket covering his legs. "At least you picked some good ones."

"I threw a couple tabloids in there too," she said dryly. "Knowing how you love gossip the way you do."

He made a face. "Turn up your nose all you want, cupcake. Readers eat it up. And without readers, you've got nothing."

She sighed a little. "How're you feeling?"

"Like I had my chest cracked open. One of the nurses scored me some reading glasses. You see them anywhere?"

She found them in the confusing mass of items crammed on top of the rolling unit where most of his wires were attached. The glasses were fluorescent pink and studded with rhinestones; she polished them quickly on the edge of her shirt and handed them to him. "Why didn't you tell anyone how bad things had gotten at the *Washtub?*"

He slid the narrow glasses onto his nose and snapped open the newspaper. "Been snooping in my business, Shea?"

"Quite honestly, I haven't really had the time," she said. "But I'm going to, first chance I get, unless you tell me first."

He sighed noisily, though the effect was pretty well ruined by the wince he gave. He pressed his hand to the thick bandages covering his entire chest as the machines beside him busily spewed out a thin strip of paper with a wildly jagged graph on it and chirped a cacophony of beeps. Worried, she waited for a nurse to come running, but no one did.

"Relax," Harvey muttered. "Been doing that all morning."

Her panic subsided. "So what do the doctors say?"

"Paper's dead. No chance of resuscitation."

"I mean about you."

"Paper's dead. No chance of resuscitation." His voice was dry as dust.

"Harvey."

He looked at her over the rims of the glasses. "Don't worry," he said. "You can walk into any publication around and hold your own. You're a good writer, cupcake. Damn good."

"You're just saying that because you're afraid I gave you mouth-to-mouth resuscitation or something."

His lips quirked. "Yeah, well. Give you something to compare against that pretty Paxton Merrick of yours."

"Maybe it was Josh who gave you the breath of life," Shea countered. "He was there, too."

"Josh wouldn't cross the street to help somebody dying on the other side."

"Harvey! That's a terrible thing to say."

He flipped open the paper. "He's a good writer, too. But not like you. Doesn't know how to put out the facts and still grab a person's heart when they least expect it."

"All these compliments are going to go to my head."

"Probably," he agreed. "You women tend to go overboard about most anything."

"You're impossible, you know that? Do you talk to the nurses here this way?"

He ignored her and flipped to the next page. And the next.

She exhaled. "All right. Is there anything you need? That you want me to bring the next time I'm here? Maybe some reading glasses that aren't sparkly and pink?"

"You don't need to keep visiting me. You've got a life, as you like to remind me."

"And you're part of it, old man, so cut the nonsense and just tell me if there's something you'd like me to bring." She gestured vaguely. "A pair of pajamas or something? I'm sure the nurses would be glad not to have to look at your hairy shoulders every minute of the day."

He smiled slightly and gingerly reached over again, nudging the stack of papers to see the nameplates. "More of these'll do."

There was no point in reminding him that he could read all of the content in digital format. He already knew and still preferred the feel of newsprint between his fingers. Frankly, she did too. She also liked to read hardbound novels and loved the smell of a library book.

"Where's your boyfriend?"

She chewed the inside of her cheek. "At the boat works." He wanted to get in some time on their latest build. She was meeting him there after she finished in Kirkland, and from there they were meeting the real estate agent. A fact that still made her quake inside. "Harvey. What about the *Tub* going strictly online? Couldn't we find a way to make it work? People still like the local stories. They like reading about their own neighborhoods. Their own schools."

He gave her a look. "Think I haven't tried, cupcake? I'm an old-school editor, Shea. Not a publisher. Not a marketing expert, and that's what half these kids are these days."

"Then find one!"

"There's no money. Nobody's going to take a pay cut when their salaries and benefits are already about as low as they can get." He sighed. "It's time. *The Seattle Washtub* had a good long run, but it's time. Got enough to put together a final issue—you can let Stu know he's responsible for it, he's the most experienced and capable enough—and that'll be that." He rubbed his hand carefully over his chest. "They tell me I've got to slow down now anyway. Less stress." He grimaced. "More *fiber*."

"Knowing your diet, I'm sure they said a lot more than that." The man lived on fast food, cigarettes and beer.

He grunted. Flipped to the next page and scanned it with his practiced eye. "Maybe I'll take up fishing."

She snorted, smiling despite everything. "I'd pay good money to see that."

He gave that some consideration and then shook his head. "Still not enough to put the *Tub* close to the black."

She sat forward and rested her folded hands on the side of the bed. "Is there anyone I can call for you?"

It was his turn to snort. "Guess I would've said the undertaker, but you made sure that wasn't necessary." He folded the paper, set it aside and pushed the ridiculous-looking glasses up to his forehead. "Don't worry about me, cupcake. I've always been better alone."

"Why?"

He eyed her. "I let the one woman I ever cared about walk away from me more than thirty years ago because it was easier than fighting to make it work. Never forgot her. Never replaced her. And never wanted to feel like that again. Instead, I stuck with what I was good at." He picked up the next paper and snapped it open. "And now it's time to move on from there, too."

"You're breaking my heart, Harvey," she murmured. And there wasn't an ounce of sarcasm in her words.

"Good you got one, kid. Don't let it dry up like a prune."

"You're too young to retire. Fish will stand up in the water and laugh at you."

"Maybe I'll take up sailing." He gave his head a jerk, and the glasses plopped down on his hawkish nose as if they'd been programmed to do so. "Rent myself a little sloop from Merrick & Sullivan Yachting."

"Pax says we should have you come to dinner."

"What the hell for?"

She rose from the chair and smiled. "So we can feed you a meal full of lots of *fiber*." Then she kissed his cheek again and picked up the chair to move it back where it belonged.

"Ehh." He grunted and snapped the newspaper again.

But he was smiling a little.

And that was enough.

Instead of driving the Audi out to Kirkland as she'd originally planned, she impetuously made her way to Cornelia's waterfront office in Ballard, wincing every time she ground the poor vehicle's gears. But at least she didn't have to contend with wet streets just yet because, so far, the day was dry.

She parked in front of the brick building, locked the car and carried the envelope full of letters inside.

"Shea!" Cornelia was standing in the foyer with Phil and gave her a surprised look. "You didn't need to come by today. How is poor Harvey?"

"Surprisingly well," she said. "I just came from visiting him at the hospital." She gestured with the manila envelope. "Do you have a few minutes to discuss these?"

"Of course." She tucked her hand through Shea's arm and they headed up one side of the grand staircase.

When they reached the top, Shea looked around in surprise. "Where's the scaffolding?"

"Painters finished on Wednesday," Cornelia said. "Thank *heavens*." Her smile was surprisingly impish. "Now if I can keep Harry busy with something else so he'll stop meddling here, things can finally settle down." She let go of Shea and turned into her office, waving smoothly at the loveseats. "Let's sit where it's more comfortable. Coffee?"

Shea's mouth watered but she shook her head. "No, thank you." She set the manila packet on the antique square coffee table between the loveseats and slipped out of her jacket before sitting down. "I'm pregnant, actually."

"Oh, I already know that." Cornelia sat down opposite her and smiled.

She absorbed that. "Pax did tell you then."

Cornelia's brows rose. "What makes you think that?"

"Then how did you know?"

She smiled gently. "I have three daughters, Shea. Only a little older than you. And *you* had the look. When you gave up the coffee here that you usually drank by the half gallon, I knew for certain. But it's your business. I knew you'd share the news when you were ready. Pax is going to be a wonderful father."

Shea's fingers nervously pleated the edge of her fake suede jacket. "Yes." She didn't have doubts on that score. He'd excel at the role just as he excelled at everything. But even though he consumed nearly every thought she had, she wasn't there to talk about him.

She leaned forward and placed her hand on the thick, bulging envelope. "I read all of the letters, Cornelia. But I think maybe you should have Phil or one of the others go through them. I didn't find anything compelling, but there might be something I didn't see."

"I doubt that. Your instincts for these things are excellent, Shea. I wish you trusted them as much as I do. But does this mean you are declining my offer?"

She shifted. "I think I should. I'm not…trained for any of this." She waved her hand, trying to describe something that defied definition.

Cornelia laughed, genuinely amused. "Do you think any of us have had any *training?*" Her eyes smiled. "I want to do something good with Harry's wedding gift to me. I want to help others who are struggling the way I once struggled. But training?" She shook her head, still laughing softly.

"You've only helped women," Shea said. "I assume that's because you have that as your basic mission."

"Well." Cornelia thought about it for a moment. "Not in so many words."

"The other aspect is matching those you help with a person possessing expertise and success or a particular skill set who can mentor them toward achieving their goal."

"Yes."

She sat forward, folding her hands together so Cornelia wouldn't see just how nervous she was. "What if—" she hesitated, wanting to frame her words exactly right "—there was a situation outside of that particular box?"

Cornelia tilted her head slightly, studying Shea's face. "Have you found yourself a Cindy you want us to help?"

Shea couldn't help but smile wryly. Harvey wouldn't appreciate being called that, but he *had* willingly worn a pair of rhinestone-studded pink reading glasses. "The *Washtub* lost its publisher," she said bluntly. "Harvey evidently tried on his own to find backers and keep it going, but as he admitted to me just this morning, he doesn't possess the expertise to guide the publication into a new business model."

"Another newspaper falls to the digital age." Cornelia's slender fingers softly drummed the arm of the loveseat. "The *Washtub* has a website, though. I've looked at it myself."

"We do. But it's not what it should be. And the paper needs to focus on competing in that medium and not so much on physical delivery twice a week to people's doorsteps." She tucked her hair behind her ear. "I'm not suggesting you finance the deal or anything. I know this is way beyond the kind of agreements you've structured with your Cindys. Not just in cost but in scope. But is there anyone you can recommend who could help show Harvey how to save what's left of the *Washtub?*"

Cornelia looked thoughtful. She rose, walked over to her table by the window and poured herself a mug of coffee. "I hope you don't mind." She lifted her cup.

"Of course not. And I understand completely if I am out of line—"

Cornelia wordlessly waved her slender hand and Shea stopped talking. She sat back and watched the other woman sip from her lovely china cup as she gazed out the windows. "I can think of a few ideas." She seemed to be talking to herself more than Shea. "What were your goals when you started out?"

She turned and looked at Shea, clearly waiting for an answer. "In journalism?" Shea smiled wryly. "A Pulitzer, of course."

"Ever envision yourself as a publisher?"

Alarm sank through Shea's chest and she shot off the loveseat. "I was never suggesting—"

"I know that." Cornelia returned to the loveseat and gestured impatiently for Shea to sit. "As you said, keeping a publication running is a larger project than normal. But that's not to say there aren't means." Her expression turned wry. "And my husband Harrison has much too much time on his hands. And too much money."

Shea swallowed, more nervous than ever. "Your husband. Mr., uh, *Hunt*."

"That is the man to whom I'm finally married," Cornelia allowed humorously. "Don't look so terrified, dear, though his reputation is admittedly well-deserved. He's no publisher, either. But he's brilliant in putting the right teams together to accomplish great things, as HuntCom proves."

"Then there'd be no need for me—"

"There's every need." Cornelia gave her a surprisingly stern look. "Someone who can keep things in line. And things—in this instance—would include Harry. He's kind of a steamroller when he gets going. But you could do it."

Shea's jaw was slack.

"I'm not saying you should dedicate your entire life to a new goal," Cornelia continued. "You're going to have a baby, and that's where you'll be focusing all of your nurturing energies. But you can carry the role of publisher without giving your life over to it as long as you have the right team. Harvey Hightower has an excellent reputation for doing what he does well and should be part of that team as long as he's willing and able."

"And that all takes money!"

"Well, yes, Shea. Money. Quite a lot of it, I'm thinking, which often makes those involved rather tense. But with the right people, with the right *heart*," she looked pointedly at her, "amazing things are possible." She lifted her shoulder casually. "Or you can refuse, naturally. Things are no worse for us tossing around the idea."

"Pax already says I work too many hours." Shea wasn't sure where the words came from. She couldn't actually be \considering the woman's suggestion, could she?

"He's right." Cornelia crossed her legs. She was wearing peach-colored slacks and a matching twinset, with a single strand of pearls around her neck. And if Shea had ever thought the woman was a pushover for a sad story, she was suddenly getting a glimpse of the iron confidence hidden beneath the soft, gentle exterior. "So let's say your hours should be limited to no more than five per day. Would that be acceptable?"

"I couldn't be a publisher in five hours a day!"

"Shea. You're guilty of what Harry is always accusing me. Not thinking *large* enough. You can do anything with the right means." Her fingers lightly drummed the loveseat arm, and the stone on her wedding ring glittered. "And I can make sure you have the means."

"And what do you get in exchange?"

"The same thing I always get," she said calmly. "Satisfaction and pleasure." She thought for a moment. "Though in this instance, my husband will insist on a portion of profit. But I suppose that's fair."

Shea's head was whirling. "I just came here with the idea of helping Harvey."

"And wouldn't this be doing that?"

"What if all he really wants is to retire? Go fishing?"

"Then he retires. He goes fishing. You'll find a job writing for another newspaper here. Or you'll come and work for me full time because that offer is always going to be on the table. I'm in no position to force anyone to agree to something that right now is simply an idea."

"I'm not supposed to be one of your Cindys," she couldn't help protesting.

"Harvey is your Cindy, dear. Is there some law that says you can't be his very own fairy godmother and still be my very own Cinderella project?"

The day had already held too much, and it wasn't even noon.

Shea blew out a shaky breath, hating that she felt tearful. Particularly after Cornelia had just told her she believed she could hold her own up against Harrison Hunt!

"At least I wouldn't have to worry about you thinking there's going to be some major romance between Harvey and me," she muttered.

Cornelia laughed merrily. "Oh, Shea, there is already a major romance going on. You're pregnant, after all."

She flushed. "But you didn't set up Pax and me in business together or anything. He just…just has an office next door. And I'd met him long before—" she waved her hand around "—all this."

Cornelia's eyes sparkled. "A happy coincidence. But I *will* expect a wedding invitation."

Shea chewed the inside of her cheek. Her eyes over-flowed.

"Oh." Cornelia tsked and moved around the table to sit beside Shea. She covered Shea's twisting hands with one of her own. "What is it? Hasn't he proposed yet? I've known that boy for years. He will, I'm certain of it."

"Oh, he's proposed all right," Shea said thickly. "More than once because of the baby." And he loved her. He'd said it. Again and again while he'd driven her body to heaven and back again. "I don't believe in marriage, Cornelia." She looked at the other woman. "My mother's done it seven times with six different men. What does it count for?"

"Hmm. We could stack up your mother's efforts against Harry's," she said wryly. "He certainly tried plenty of times himself and always with the most horrible women." She shuddered a little. "Take your mother's experiences out of the equation, Shea. They don't have to be yours. And I don't even have to ask if you love him."

Shea jerked. She hadn't admitted anything of the sort. Not even to herself.

"It's written all over your face, dear, every time you say his name."

She looked down and blinked hard.

Cornelia patted her hand again and rose, returning a moment later with a tissue that she tucked into Shea's fist. "Don't think about marriage. Perhaps what you might ask yourself instead is whether you believe in *commitment*. Because that's what it takes to make a family work."

"Excuse me." Phil knocked softly on the opened door, drawing their attention. "I'm sorry to interrupt, but Laurie Schaeffer is here to go over the terms of her contract. I've put her in the conference room."

Cornelia glanced at the narrow diamond watch on her wrist. "I'll be right there, Phil. Thank you." She waited until the other woman had left the doorway and then gave Shea's hands a squeeze before rising. "Take as much time here as you need. But please. Think about what I said."

"The *Tub* doesn't have much time for me to sit around and think."

Cornelia tsked again. She caught Shea's chin in her hand as if she were five. "The *Tub* is just a business, Shea." Her eyes were kind but as serious as Shea had ever seen them. "I'm talking about your *life*. I've known Harry since we were children, but it took us nearly a lifetime before we finally got it right. You're still young. Spend your lifetime *with* the one you love. Don't let that opportunity pass you by just because you're afraid."

Chapter Fourteen

Shea sat in the Audi, her hands clenching and unclenching around the steering wheel, and stared at the enormous building in front of her.

She'd driven the short distance from Cornelia's office to Merrick & Sullivan Boat Works and everywhere she looked, there were boats. In the water. Out of the water. But through the yawning, industrial-sized doorway that was wide open to the day, she could see only shadows.

She hadn't called Pax to tell him she was coming early. Hadn't called to say a word about her conversation with Harvey. Or the truly mind-boggling one with Cornelia.

She just needed to see him. Talk to him. Find out if he thought the plan was as crazy as it had to be.

As for everything else Cornelia had said—

Her mind shied away from it.

She blew out a breath, parked the car next to Pax's SUV in the lot and walked toward the building. The closer she got, the larger it became, reminding her oddly of an airplane hangar. There didn't seem to be any sort of regular office entrance, so she entered through the gigantic doorway and was immediately surrounded by noise and the scent of wood.

A few men stood beneath the skeleton of what someday would be a truly immense sailboat. They wore hard hats and tool belts and held ropes that reached over pulleys high in the metal beams near the roof, then back down again to the massive wooden pieces being slowly inched into place by a crane. It, too, was dwarfed by the structure.

Her fingers actually itched for a camera, so impressive was the sight.

Then a figure appeared on the inside of the framework. Pax was well over six feet, but even he looked small in comparison to the behemoth surrounding him. He was gesturing broadly with outstretched hands at the crane and beam overhead, and she could hear him yelling but didn't understand the terms. She only knew she was watching something magnificent and wondered why on earth she hadn't asked him to show her the heart of his and Erik's operation earlier. And then, as if he sensed her, he suddenly turned on his heel and smiled across at her.

And everything in her went still.

And calm.

She lifted her hand in a silent wave and he pointed to the metal stairs off to one side that led up to a catwalk. She realized that was where the office was and nodded, heading that way.

She stopped partway up, her hand wrapped around the metal pipe handrail, and watched them again, trying to imagine what the various angles and shapes would end up forming on the finished product.

"Come check out the photos," an amused voice came

from above, and she looked up to see Erik leaning over the catwalk rail. He was dressed in work clothes, too, minus the hard hat. He gestured at the walls behind him. "If you want to see more of what we do."

She eagerly ascended the rest of the stairs and saw a series of offices, all lined with windows that overlooked the production area below. Not unlike Harvey's window that looked out on the newsroom, she thought whimsically. "Sorry to come by unannounced," she said a little breathlessly when she reached the top. She gazed out over the view. "This is incredible."

Erik's eyes crinkled. "Makes coming to the office pretty enjoyable. And you hardly need to worry about announcing yourself. Pax told me the two of you were going house hunting today. About time he grew up and got a backyard of his own."

She laughed. "I think he's pretty grown up even without the yard."

Erik grinned and jerked his head. "Come on. I'll show you Pax's office."

She followed him through one of the doorways toward the center of the catwalk and he gestured at the pearl-gray wall, where dozens of black-and-white photographs were mounted, showing boats under construction. "Those show most stages every M & S boat goes through," he said.

"I've only been on *Honey Girl* once," she admitted, moving over to study the blown-up images more closely. "She's so beautiful, but it's hard to imagine the steps that went into creating her."

"He used to say *Honey* was the only girl he loved." Erik sat on the corner of the metal desk that took up much less floor space than the large drafting table next to it did. "He never said it again once you came along." He picked up a framed photograph on the desk and turned it so she could see.

She frowned and took it out of his hands. It was a snapshot of her and Pax from Erik and Rory's wedding reception. Pax was holding out his hand to her when he'd asked her to dance.

His expression was caught clearly and her heart squeezed.

She slowly set the frame back on Pax's desk. "The most obvious things are right in front—" They both jerked when there was a loud crash.

Erik bolted toward the catwalk rail, looking down. And then he swore. "Stay here," he ordered tersely and ran toward the stairs.

Shea's heart climbed into her throat as she followed, stopping at the rail to look down from the dizzying height.

Shouts and curses floated up from the production floor and her eyes anxiously sought out Pax amid the cloud of dust that was rising right along with the shouts. But she couldn't see him.

Not even aware of moving, she was suddenly racing down the steps, the flat heels of her boots clanging against the metal, but when she reached the ground and would have tried to go closer to the skeleton of the boat, an arm came around her waist, hauling her back.

"Where do you think you're going?"

She looked up into Pax's face.

Below the hard hat, dust caked his cheeks and jaw, and his clothes were nearly white with it. "God," she cried, relief like she'd never known making her weak. She clamped her hands on his face and hauled him down to her, pressing her mouth to his, feeling the graininess covering his lips. "I was so afraid," she mumbled against him.

The iron band of his grip turned gentle and he slipped

his palm up her back. He kissed her softly. "Been there," he said once he straightened again. Then he made a face. "Dammit, don't do that." He brushed his thumbs over her cheeks. "You know I can't take it when you do that."

She hadn't even known she was crying. Her hands shook as she did her own touching. Over his chest, swiping away dust. Over his wide shoulders, his hair-roughened forearms and his face yet again. "You're not hurt?"

"No. I'm not hurt." He thumbed back his hard hat, revealing a band of clean, suntanned skin, and raised his voice. "No thanks to Jake," he yelled loudly, "because he still hasn't learned how to tie a bloody knot! A kindergartner could've done better!"

A chorus of laughter and jeers rose through the cloud of dust that was still rolling outward.

Shea pressed her head weakly to the center of his chest, trying to ignore images of that huge wooden beam crashing down from the crane. He'd been standing beneath it when she'd arrived. "I would die if something happened to you."

"Whoa, whoa, whoa." He lifted her chin and his brown eyes searched hers. "Nothing's going to happen to me."

"But if something did—"

"But nothing did. Or will. Not until I've had a lifetime with you."

Her heart was smashed into dust finer than the cloud beyond him. "I love you." The words burst out of her. "I love you, and I don't care if you only want to marry me because of the baby. I don't care that it's the only reason you fell in love with me or—"

He hauled her off her feet and pressed his mouth to hers. Long and hard and well.

And when he finally set her back on her feet, she realized that his crew was hooting at them now.

He waved his arm dismissively and tugged her out into the sunlight and away from their view.

"Pax, I—"

"Be quiet." He pressed his hands on his lean hips and looked around at the parking lot. "This is a helluva place," he murmured, then grabbed her hand again. "Come on."

"But I need to—"

"Just wait. Okay? Humor me for a few minutes. This is not what I planned."

Confused, she had to trot behind him to keep up with his long strides as he pulled her with him past the building and down to the maze of docks. And finally, she realized their destination. *Honey Girl* sat gently swaying at the end of a floating pier. "Her mainsail's under repair or I'd take her out," he said when they reached her. He lightly hopped across to the deck and hauled on the rope tying her to the pier, closing the gap of water by several feet.

She knew it wasn't as easy as he made it look, simply because she could see the tendons in his forearms standing out. But he stayed steady and set one foot back on the pier, straddling the water below. "Put your foot there." He gestured, then held out his hand. "Take my hand and just step across. I won't let you fall."

She slid her hand in his and felt his fingers close around it. The pier was narrow and moved far more than she was used to. But she put her foot where he said. And stepped across. Because he wasn't going to let her fall.

Then he pushed away from the pier and stepped into the boat, lifting her beyond the rail and onto the deck.

"Pax—"

"Just hold on." He flipped open a bench and pulled out a cushion that matched the upholstery she remembered from the cabin bunk and set it on the bench. "Now. You can sit."

She sat.

"You want a life vest? I've got plenty of them."

Feeling strangely lightheaded, she shook her head. "I'm not exactly in danger of falling overboard from here," she said faintly. "Besides, you'd catch me."

"Yes," he said quietly. "I would."

It was nowhere near as noisy as it had been in the boat works, but there was still plenty going on. Birds cawing, horns blowing and water slapping against the sides of the boats. But when he looked at her the way he was, his eyes warm and gentle, the only thing she really heard was her heart beating inside her head.

"How was Harvey?"

It was the last thing she expected him to ask. "Fine. Really much better than I expected him to be." She searched his eyes. "Cornelia seems to think she has an idea how to help him keep the *Tub* afloat."

"Good for her."

She pushed nervously to her feet. "Well, it kind of involves me, too. She...she thinks maybe I could be publisher."

His eyebrows rose.

"With a lot of help," she added rapidly, "from, you know, experts who *would* know what to really do. And her husband. Because he's the real money."

"Is that something you're interested in doing?"

She chewed the inside of her lip. "I don't know. Maybe." She realized she was pressing her hands to her belly. "Is it...crazy? To think about something like that when we're going to have a baby in September?"

"It's only crazy if you end up doing too much. I told you once that you didn't have to work if you didn't want to."

"I know." Which just brought her around to what she needed to say. "I never wanted to love anyone, Pax." Her eyes suddenly burned. "Certainly not the kind of man I'd convinced myself that you were. But you're not what I thought. You're not who I thought." She moistened her lips. "You're kind. And you're decent and honest. A lot more honest than I've ever been, and I meant it when I said I didn't want to hurt you. If marriage is what you want so this baby has your name, then I'll marry you. Because I love you. And I—" she swallowed and sniffed "—I just want to be with you. However that happens."

His chest rose and fell in a deep, deep sigh.

Then he closed his hands around hers and nudged her back onto the bench. He let her go and stuck one hand in his pocket. "I think I fell in love with you the first time we met," he said softly. "It had nothing to do with the baby. And although there's not a cell inside me that regrets we made him, it's a heck of an ironic note that he's the one getting in the way of the truth."

He suddenly went down on his knees in front of her until their faces were even. "I love Fig, Shea." He pulled his hand from his pocket and held it up between them. "But I have always loved you first."

A ring sat perched on the end of his little finger. The diamond, surrounded by smaller, watery blue stones, glittered and sparkled even more because his hand was actually shaking.

She pressed her fingers over her lips. "It's beautiful," she whispered.

"I bought this for you after Erik and Rory's wedding but there's been a part of me that knew I wanted you as my wife long before that. Long before you told me Fig was on the way. But you weren't exactly cooperative, sweetheart, and gave me no sort of chance to…woo…you." His lips twisted wryly.

She bit her lip, looking into his eyes.

"By Valentine's Day I was getting desperate. So I

stooped to using your cat. It's not my proudest moment, but—"

She leaned forward and kissed him silent. "But it worked," she whispered. "Marsha-Marsha loved the toys. And I love you."

He cupped the back of her head and pressed his forehead against hers. "I was going to give you the ring last night. After dinner. Somewhere dressy. Romantic. Properly, the way Bea's been lecturing me."

"Give me the ring now," she said huskily. "Give it to me and I promise I will never, ever take it off."

He let go of her and took her hand. He slid the ring into place, then he turned her palm upward and pressed his lips to it before settling it against the center of his chest, right in the same spot where she'd pressed so hard on Harvey's chest just yesterday.

But she could feel Pax's heart beating hard against her hand. Hard and sure and steady.

Just like he was.

"Thank you for loving me," she whispered. "For showing me how to believe."

His eyes gleamed. He brushed his hand over her hair. Cupped her cheek and rubbed his thumb slowly over her lips. "Thank you for finally letting me," he whispered and kissed her so sweetly she melted.

She didn't know what would happen with the *Washtub*. Whether it would fade into fond memories for those who'd read her, or whether she'd find new life. With or without Shea along for the ride.

But she did know that whatever happened, it would be okay. Because Pax wasn't going to let her fall. And if there ever were some reason that she did, he'd be there to catch her.

Always.

She wrapped her arms around his shoulders tightly. "Take me below?"

He gave her a surprised look.

Then a slow grin crossed his face.

He pushed to his feet, took her hand and led the way.

Epilogue

December

From the balcony that circled the grand reception hall at the Hunt family home located on Lake Washington, Shea stared down at the eighteen-foot Christmas tree that held court in the room below. "It's not exactly little, is it?"

Pax laughed softly. "You've been working with Harry for months now. Do you really think he ever does anything little?"

She made a face. Up until now, she'd either met with the tall, gangly man at the *Tub*'s office, at Cornelia's office or at the corner office Harry still kept at the HuntCom's corporate complex. "True," she admitted ruefully. It had taken her a full month after striking their deal before she'd had the guts to speak her mind to the intimidating old man. Cornelia's warning that her husband could be a steamroller hadn't been misplaced. But when he'd kept insisting that the *Tub* was beyond help and she'd stomped her foot and accused him of not being the visionary everyone said, he'd barked out a laugh, nodded approvingly, and told her to call him Harry instead of Mr. Hunt.

From that day on, the *Tub* had been on a bullet train toward a new life.

Changes at the paper, though, had seemed small potatoes in comparison to the changes for her and Pax.

She smiled a little, turning from the festively decorated tree and Cornelia and Harry's guests below to look at her husband of less than a week.

They'd been married in a small ceremony in the same church as Erik and Rory, on the anniversary of the ice storm, and she couldn't imagine a more perfect wedding day.

She couldn't imagine a more perfect life.

She and Pax had already made the rounds among Cornelia and Harry's guests. All of their respective daughters and sons and their spouses were there, as well as the staff of FGI and the *Tub*. And all of them combined made up only a fraction of the total guests present. "Can't believe Harvey had the nerve to go to Hawaii for the holiday and miss all this."

"Maybe he wants to work on his tan."

She grinned wryly. "Maybe."

Pax's finger slowly trailed down the back of her bare neck and she shivered.

Even though she was now a married woman, the publisher of the *Tub* and the mother of a healthy three-month-old baby boy, she'd still had to borrow a dress from her mother suitable for the Hunt's annual Christmas ball. Gloria hadn't quite forgiven her yet for making her a grandmother before she was ready, but she was coming around. Mostly because she got a kick out of Jonathan telling her she looked young enough to be the baby's mother.

She reached up and toyed with the collar of Pax's white shirt. "Think it would be rude if we left already?"

His lips tilted. "Missing Fig already?"

Fig—actually Finn Isaac Merrick—was spending the night with Pax's parents, who wouldn't be returning the baby until morning. "Yes." It was startling how completely their brown-eyed baby boy had wrapped them around his infant fingers. "But this is the first night out we've had without him since he was born."

Pax's eyes crinkled and his gaze felt like a caress. "We could always do something shocking," his voice dropped a notch, "and go...home."

She moistened her lips, feeling her stomach swoop around and suspecting it would always be that way whenever he gave her that look. "And what would we do there?"

"I can think of a thing or two."

They were in the midst of renovating their waterfront home. And even though it was located only a few blocks from her mother's house, Shea had known the second they'd seen the property that it was the perfect place for their growing family. It even came complete with a slip large enough for *Honey Girl*. "Does it involve painting the hall bathroom?"

He laughed softly and tugged on her long ponytail. "Not tonight."

She rose up on her toes and brushed her mouth over his. "I love you, Mr. Merrick."

She felt his smile against her lips and his hands circled her waist. "I love you, Mrs. Merrick."

She shivered again. "I just have one request," she added.

"Anything."

"I get to take off The Shirt."

* * * * *

Be sure not to miss other books in
THE HUNT FOR CINDERELLA *series, including*
HOLIDAY BY DESIGN by Patricia Kay
HER HOLIDAY PRINCE CHARMING by Christine Flynn
Available from Harlequin Special Edition!

#2317 LASSOED BY FORTUNE
The Fortunes of Texas: Welcome to Horseback Hollow
by Marie Ferrarella

Liam Jones doesn't want any part of newfound Fortune relatives—or the changes they bring to Horseback Hollow. *He's crazy,* thinks Julia Tierney. The ambitious beauty was always the one Liam could never snag in high school. When Julia becomes the chef at a local restaurant, Julia and Liam find that old attractions die hard....

#2318 THE DADDY SECRET
Return to Brighton Valley • by Judy Duarte

When Mallory Dickinson gave up her son, she never thought she'd see Brighton Valley—or her baby's father, Rick Martinez—again. A decade later, she's back in town with her son, whom she adopted—and Rick's become a responsible veterinarian. Can the former bad boy and the social worker let their guards down to allow love in?

#2319 A PROPOSAL AT THE WEDDING
Bride Mountain • by Gina Wilkins

Father-of-the-bride Paul Brennan can't help but find himself tempted by irresistible innkeeper Bonnie Carmichael. Trouble arises, though, since Bonnie hopes to create a life and family at Bride Mountain Inn, and Paul's already done fatherhood. In the shadow of Bride Mountain, love blooms as they find their way to a happily-ever-after.

#2320 FINDING FAMILY...AND FOREVER?
The Bachelors of Blackwater Lake • by Teresa Southwick

Kidnapped as a child, Emma Robbins heads to Blackwater Lake to find her birth family. In the process, she becomes the nanny to Dr. Justin Flint's young son. The handsome widower is unwillingly attracted to the lovely newcomer, who loves the boy as her own, but secrets and lies may undermine the family they begin to build.

#2321 HER ACCIDENTAL ENGAGEMENT • by Michelle Major

Single mom Julia Morgan needs a man—not for love, but to keep custody of her son, Charlie. Local police chief Sam Callahan wants to keep his family out of his love life. The two engage in a romance of convenience, but what begins as a pretense might just evolve into true love.

#2322 THE ONE HE'S BEEN LOOKING FOR • by Joanna Sims

World-renowned photographer Ian Sterling is going blind, and he wants to find the model of his dreams before he loses his sight entirely. He finds his muse in rebellious Jordan Brand, but there's more than a camera between these two. To truly heal, Ian must open his heart to see what's been in front of him all along.

REQUEST YOUR FREE BOOKS!
2 FREE NOVELS PLUS 2 FREE GIFTS!

H HARLEQUIN®

SPECIAL EDITION
Life, Love & Family

HSE13R

Mallory took a deep breath, probably trying to gather her thoughts—or maybe to lie.

But it didn't take a brain surgeon to see the truth. She'd kept the baby she was supposed to have given up for adoption, and she'd let ten years go by without telling Rick.

Betrayal gnawed at his gut.

"Lucas called you a doctor," she said, arching a delicate brow.

"I'm a veterinarian. My clinic is just down the street."

As she mulled that over, Lucas sidled up to Rick wearing a bright-eyed grin. "Did you come to ask my mom about Buddy?"

No, the dog was the last thing he'd come to talk to Mallory about. And while he hadn't been sure just how the conversation was going to unfold when he arrived, it had just taken a sudden and unexpected turn.

"Why would he come to talk to me about his dog?" Mallory asked her son.

Or rather *their* son. Who else could the boy be?

Lucas, who wore a smile that indicated he was completely oblivious to the tension building between the adults, approached Mallory. "Because Buddy needs a home. Since we have a yard now, can I have him? *Please?* I promise to take care of him and walk him and everything."

She said, "We'll talk about it later."

"Okay. Thanks." He flashed Rick a smile, then turned and headed toward the stairs.

As Lucas was leaving, Rick's gaze traveled from the boy to Mallory and back again. Finally, when they were alone, Rick folded his arms across his chest, shifted his weight to one hip and smirked.

"Cute kid," he said.

Mallory flushed brighter still, and she wiped her palms along her hips.

Nervous, huh? Rick's internal B.S. detector slipped into overdrive.

Well, she ought to be.

When Rick had found out about her pregnancy, he'd been only seventeen, but he'd offered to quit school, get a job and marry her. However, her grandparents had decided that she was too young and convinced her that adoption was the only way to go. So they'd sent her to Boston to live with her aunt Carrie until the birth.

Yet in spite of what she'd promised him when she left, she hadn't come back to Brighton Valley. And within six months' time, he'd lost all contact with her—through no fault of his own.

Apparently, she'd had a change of heart about the adoption. And about the feelings she'd claimed she'd had for him, too.

***

Enjoy this sneak peek from USA TODAY *bestselling author Judy Duarte's* THE DADDY SECRET, *the first book in* RETURN TO BRIGHTON VALLEY, *a brand-new miniseries coming in March 2014!*